Common Ground

A Margaret of Milton Story

Elaine Owen

Dedication

With love to my late mother-in-law, Margaret "Peggy" Holmes, who went to be with the Lord in 1999. The interaction between Hannah and Margaret Hale in chapter eleven of this story is patterned on words she said to me on the day of my marriage to her son. She was the kindest and most gracious mother-in-law a new bride could have ever hoped for, and still miss her and think of her every day. This is for you, "Mommers."

Table of Contents

Chapter One

"Call Me John"

The northbound train moved towards Milton much too quickly for John Thornton, who, in his current state of perfect happiness, wanted to savor these few hours with Margaret Hale as much as he could.

"Soon to be Margaret Thornton," he thought, allowing his lips to caress her forehead again. Margaret's actions at Marlborough Mills on the day of the riot had been ambiguous, misunderstood as sentiment for him instead of the act of contrition and protection it had been. But now--with her affectionate caresses and kisses freely bestowed on him in a public setting--they were as good as engaged. Still, the words needed to be said. There was another topic to settle first, however.

"Your brother," John murmured into Margaret's ear as her head reclined on his shoulder, his arm close about her. "Tell me about your brother."

"You know about Frederick?" Margaret's eyes, so near to his, looked up with surprise. He could easily lose himself in those blue depths, now filled with warmth that was only for him.

"Higgins mentioned him. That was him with you at the Outwood station that night, was it not?" At her answering nod, he looked away in shame. "Forgive me, Margaret, for ever doubting you. You tried to tell me all was not as it appeared. You tried to tell me not to judge."

"I could not tell you about Frederick, then. He was caught up in a mutiny at sea and although his actions may have been right before God they will never be right in the eyes of the law."

"But your father--he never even mentioned having a son!"

"It was too painful, I think," Margaret said, her eyes misting at the memory. "He missed Frederick so that even to think of him, let alone speak of him, was inexpressibly painful. We only spoke of him rarely."

"And Frederick came to see your mother?"

"Yes, as she lay dying. It was her last wish."

Thornton pressed the hand that was enveloped within his own, feeling it tremble a little at her painful memory. "I wish you had been able to tell me about him when I asked you for an explanation of your conduct."

"I could not do so. You were--and are--a magistrate. You had your duty."

"But surely you know I could never betray your trust! Besides my feelings for you, your father was my friend."

"It was not a question of trusting you, but of making you choose between your friendship and your sworn responsibilities. I would not bring that on your head."

"You might have said something later," Thornton said, still feeling the sting of her lack of faith in him.

"You had made your feelings for me plain, and I honored you for them. I would have been disappointed if you had felt otherwise. But that is all in the past now, I hope. You said you were only looking to the future," Margaret reminded him of his own words.

"Will that future be spent with you, Margaret?" Thornton asked as he gazed down at her, his voice betraying the anxiety he could not yet banish.

"It will, if you want it to," Margaret answered. It was her turn to look away in shame. "Please forgive me, Mr. Thornton, for ever misunderstanding the kind of man you are, for judging you when I knew no better, for failing to see--" She was stopped in her litany by the luminous look on Thornton's face, his mouth in a tenuous half smile.

"Call me John," he said softly.

She took a breath and began again. "Forgive me--John--for the uncaring way I answered you when you offered yourself to me--" He stopped her again.

"Just say John," he said again, as quietly as before. "That is all I need to hear from you. Say my name, and all is well."

"Dearest John!" she answered, caressing his face with her hand, and his smile widened and grew more certain as he leaned down to kiss her again.

"Marry me, Margaret," said Thornton, when they next paused for speech. "I want us to marry as soon as possible."

"Yes, John," she answered, and the train traveled on completely unnoticed by the two inhabitants of one particular car.

Chapter Two

"Welcome Home"

The train was only minutes from Milton before Margaret began to give more serious consideration to the practical difficulties that lay before her.

"I changed plans so quickly when I came with you that I have given no thought at all to my lodgings. Where shall I stay in Milton? The house I shared with my parents is no longer available, of course."

"Nothing could be simpler," Thornton answered at once. "You will stay in our home until we are married."

"My dear, I do not think that will serve at all," Margaret objected. "I had much better take a room in a hotel."

"Where I cannot protect you? I will not allow it. You must stay with mother and me. If it is propriety that worries you, my mother's maid shall stay in your room."

"Thank you, John. You are most considerate. But it is not merely propriety that occupies me. I should like to be separate from you for at least a few days before the wedding so that . . . so that . . ." her voice trailed off.

"So that why?" Thornton asked, perplexed.

"So that we may come together again on that day." She blushed furiously as she said this, and Thornton marveled again at the beauty that would be his to adore whenever he wished once they were married.

"And then we will never separate again," he said quietly, allowing his thumb to caress the palm of one hand that rested in his so delicately.

"When will that be? Do you wish to be married from Helstone? Or will Milton serve?"

"Helstone is part of my past. I wish only to look forward, away from the sadness of these past two years. If I were to have my choice, then I choose to be married in Milton." As she spoke, Margaret remembered the wish she had expressed to Henry Lennox so long before, of walking to the church on her wedding day down a wooded lane, with green trees on every side. That dream seemed faded now, like a favorite dress that has lost its color and been pushed aside. The reality of the man before her, strong, steady, and kind, brilliantly outshone her previous wish and made it fade away into nothingness.

"And when can our marriage take place? I assure you that I will try to be patient, to accommodate your needs, but it is not a trait that comes easily to me. Tell me that we will come together soon; or is it important to you to have a large wedding?"

"Perhaps," said Margaret, "we should speak to your mother first. She may not be willing to go along with a wedding in a short time. She might need time to get used to the idea of me marrying you at all."

"My mother," said Thornton, allowing his eyes to lock adoringly with hers, "is going to love you."

∞

These days Hannah Thornton was thinking frequently of Margaret Hale in the strongest possible terms, and those thoughts were not always loving ones. There were times, in fact, when she thought she might hate the girl.

A mother's love is a proud and jealous thing, and the only thing that a proud mother might resent more than a girl who steals her only son's affection is a girl who steals it without giving him her affection in return. If a mother must lose her son's heart to another woman, she at least wants that woman to be worthy of its possession. Margaret Hale had been weighed in the balance, and found wanting.

It was Margaret's southern upbringing, Hannah thought, which had poisoned everything from the start. A northern girl, accustomed to following the fortunes and pitfalls of commerce, would have known who John Thornton was. She would have appreciated his character and understood the hard choices he had to make every day. She would have admired his fortitude and sharp business sense, and been only too flattered to be the recipient of his heartfelt adoration, even if her own heart was not touched in return. If she must decline, then she would do so gently.

But these southern girls! Oh! The airs they gave themselves, the proud condescending looks, the presumption to tell a man like her son how he ought to run his business! How interfering, how very knowing they were on subjects of which they knew nothing at all.

To be fair, Hannah reminded herself, Margaret was the first southern girl she had ever come to know well. Perhaps they were not all like that. But it hardly mattered. Margaret Hale was, and she had broken John's heart, and Hannah would never be able to forgive her for it.

At least, that was how she had felt until she came upon Margaret unexpectedly in the empty workroom of Marlborough Mills, after John had closed his business forever. She, Hannah, had pulled her own pride about her like a suit of armor and aimed several barbs straight at the younger woman, expecting to have them thrown back at her. Instead, Margaret had responded with an unexpected kindness and humility. Perhaps there had even been regret there. There had certainly been compassion, and a tenderness visible when Margaret pressed on Hannah's arm at the mention of her son's devotion. Thinking back on it now, as she sat restlessly by the fireplace on this cloudy day, she had to admit that Margaret Hale had depths to her that she, Hannah, had never before appreciated. If Margaret harbored her own regrets, Hannah harbored even more. A small voice of doubt had begun to speak in her mind.

Perhaps she had judged too quickly. After all, Margaret had not tried to deceive Hannah, to pretend that she had not been seen at the Outwood station that night, nor had she grown angry with Hannah for rebuking her for indiscretion, at least not at first. What had she said, exactly? Hannah frowned as she tried to recall. *"I have done wrong, but not in the way you imagine."* The puzzling words seemed to confirm the dark hints John had given, that Margaret had been in some kind of trouble. Could it be that the trouble was not of Margaret's own making? But John would probably have said if that were the case. Nevertheless, she promised herself that if she ever saw Margaret again, she would not judge her again before hearing the whole story, once and for all.

But this would not do! This painful brooding would not serve! She shook off the melancholy that threatened to drag her down as she stood from her chair and mentally inventoried the tasks she must continue to work on before John returned from wherever he had gone. He had left only a week before, and since she had received no word from him, Hannah assumed he would be back any day now. She was on the lookout for a small, comfortable home which she and John could rent once they quit Marlborough Mills entirely. Once the house was picked out, furniture would have to be sorted through as well, with some pieces being moved along with their personal items and others being sold outright. Fanny's room, replete with ornate bric-a-brac and useless ornaments, would have to be emptied completely. Clothing would need to be sorted through as well, with special attention given to certain simpler items not worn much when John Thornton had been a master. They would probably also have to give up a servant or two. Yes, there were many changes ahead, and it was time that Hannah Thornton faced them head on.

When the blast of the train sounded later that afternoon, the sound breaking through even her preoccupied perusal of the household linens, Hannah barely paid attention. Trains may come and trains may go, but the work of managing a home stayed ever the same. Many trains had traveled through the station since John had left and she had not the patience to wonder if he was on every one of them. Her first notice of John's return would most likely be a delivery man bearing his bags, and so she listened half-heartedly for a porter's quick step and a rap on their door while she picked through bed sheets. When half an hour had gone by she thought no more of it.

At half past four Hannah stood up to stretch after the tedium of folding innumerable table runners, napkins, and other linens. It was almost time for tea; the maid would summon her soon. She looked out into the yard that opened on to the mill, fascinated, as always, to watch the stream of humanity that flowed past her home at shift change every day. The great looms of Marlborough Mills were silent, but the employees of other factories, both men and women, hurried by in their heavy boots and rough clothes, their work-calloused hands clutching tins and bags closely as they went on their way. Here a young girl kept a quick pace with her father; there a mother and child walked together to their shift, sharing a bite of apple each as they went. Each was as oblivious to each other as they were to her, not even glancing up as they went by, intent on their destinations. There were so many, all in nondescript tones of blue and gray, that they formed an unbroken wave that swirled through the courtyard like small currents and eddies in a larger stream.

In the distance, at the end of the yard, a small opening appeared, an almost unnoticeable gap in the unrelenting blue and gray. A slash of black appeared, coming through the archway slowly but determinedly, in a straight line towards the house where Hannah now stood at the window, looking out. John's clothes were black and so was his hair, which made him easy to pick out even when cut off from Hannah's sight for moments at a time by the people passing in front of him.

Beside him walked a smaller, slender figure in a familiar green-striped calico and a rich brown merino hat that contrasted strongly with the severity of the harsher colors around her. This much Hannah could see only through the briefest of glimpses as a small crowd of workers began to move in front of the advancing figures. But it was enough for her to recognize the dainty but sturdy form, the upright bearing, the graceful, sweeping glance that took in everything in her surroundings. Hannah tightened her lips as she watched.

The procession--for such it had become--had come to a virtual stop about thirty feet from the front of the house. A small crowd of mill workers had surrounded John and Margaret, a crowd that grew as each person pointed out the couple's arrival to the person next to them. Nicholas Higgins was standing near Margaret, carrying two carpet bags and speaking warmly to her and John. He had accompanied them into the yard, but Hannah had not noticed him before. Now he stood as a kind of gatekeeper, allowing only one person at a time to approach closely. Rough men with weather-beaten faces were pressing John's hand firmly. Mothers with children were pressing forward and greeting Margaret, who smiled on them all with the unfeigned warmth that only she seemed able to generate.

Margaret looked up briefly, once, as the crowd flowed in front her, and her eyes met Hannah's through the glass of the living room window. Her eyes flared wide with recognition; she smiled, and then her face relaxed into the marvelous serenity that Hannah had noted before. No matter how tumultuous her circumstances, Margaret had always seemed to carry an air of simple peace about her.

Hannah began to notice other things as well. When Margaret glanced away from Hannah's sharp gaze, her eyes dropped briefly, and then swept up to look adoringly at the man next to her--at John. There was a shy, proud affection in that look which Hannah had never seen before, and also in the answering look that John gave her. John reached one hand up to cover and press on Margaret's hand, which lay on his arm in a familiar way, and he leaned down to speak intimately in Margaret's ear. Margaret's smile never wavered as she nodded in agreement with whatever John had said and looked back at him again with that same affectionate expression. They resumed their advance towards the house.

These gestures were not the interactions of business acquaintances or casual friends. They spoke of ease, freedom, and a closeness between the two that was as fresh as it was dear. John and Margaret had left

Milton separately, but they had returned as one.

Hannah turned her keen observation from Margaret to John, who had kept his hand on top of Margaret's as they walked together towards the steps of the house. His head, always held high, was higher now than ever, and it seemed to Hannah that several deep lines of worry she had grown accustomed to seeing lately on his forehead had disappeared. When had that happened, she wondered. When had his steps become so lively, so full of quick grace? When had the dimmed, anxious look in his eyes been replaced with this joyous tenderness? He was still John, still her beloved son, but she felt as though she were seeing him for the first time when he had the obvious affection of the woman he loved finally returned to him.

Hannah felt her resentment towards Margaret fading, disappearing as quickly as water evaporating on a hot stone.

She moved towards the front door and opened it just as John and Margaret climbed the steps, Higgins directly behind them. The rest of the scene faded away as Hannah took in the two young people looking at her--John, with a new, manly air of pride and responsibility, and Margaret with her affection on delicate display. A thousand words came to Hannah's mind, but she stood tongue tied for a moment, a small smile beginning to break through, until the only words that mattered finally came to her lips and sprang forth--

"Welcome home."

Chapter Three

A Man's Pride

My dear Edith,

I am writing to you from Milton, where Henry has probably told you that I went yesterday. I am terribly sorry not to have returned to London and you, but you see I could never go away from Milton again, after I met Mr. Thornton by chance on the railway platform and discovered that he still loves me.

Yes, he loves me, Edith! Despite my mistaken prejudices against him and the north, regardless of my cruel words to him when he proposed the first time--he loved me then, and he loves me still. And I love him so very much. I could not come back to London, Edith, once I realized that my heart was always here. Please console Henry as best you can. I know that at one point he cherished his own notions towards me. I should not like him to be hurt.

Mr. Thornton and I have decided to be married in two weeks' time. I am staying at Marlborough Mills until a few days before then, when I should like to have you and the captain arrive if you can. We can all take rooms in the G----- Hotel together and then, I hope the captain will agree to give me away at the Milton church. Please say that you will come. I want you to meet John and see for yourself the goodness of the man who has completely won me by his noble and compassionate nature.

Eagerly awaiting your answer, I am

Your loving cousin,

Margaret Hale

"How will the two of you occupy yourselves today?" Thornton asked at breakfast the next day, his smile showing his profound delight at the inclusion of Margaret in the intimate family group.

"We will begin preparing wedding clothes," Hannah answered decisively. "You and Margaret may want only a small wedding, but it will still be as dignified as possible. I owe it to your mother, my dear," she added, speaking to Margaret, "to see that you are cared for in this matter just as you would have been if she were still here. You may rest assured that no detail will be overlooked." Margaret smiled her gratitude.

"We will also," Hannah added dryly, "call on Fanny and let her know your news, if Margaret is willing. No doubt she will believe that Margaret came all this way simply to see the glory of her Indian wallpaper, but we will inform her otherwise."

All three laughed before Margaret gained the courage to shyly ask, "And what will you do today--John?" blushing furiously as she did so.

Thornton hesitated momentarily. "I have an appointment quite early this morning, with a gentleman who may be offering me a position where I can make a respectable salary for myself."

"John!" This was from Hannah, spoken in shock. She abruptly set down the pitcher of cream she had been holding. She knew, of course, of the wealth which Margaret had inherited so unexpectedly, and of the role it had played in bringing Margaret together with her son. It had all been explained to her the night before. Margaret said nothing, but she looked at John with wide-eyed concern.

"You will not be a master again?" Hannah demanded.

Thornton took a deep breath, preparing himself for opposition. "No, mother, not at this time. I am not minded to use my wife's money for my own business interests. It will be better if I work hard for a few years, set aside my own earnings, and then begin again, on my own, just as I did before."

"I do not agree!" Margaret said strongly, startling even herself. "I meant what I said to you yesterday. I mean to invest in your business, in Marlborough Mills."

"My love, you have no need of my poor skills," Thornton answered with a tender smile. "You have more than enough to keep you comfortably for the rest of your life. You need not risk any of the principal. If you must invest, let it be with a well-established business somewhere else. It will take me some time to save enough to start my own business again, and in the meantime, my venture would be too risky."

"But I want to invest my money with you! There is no need to wait to save your own money when everything I have will soon be yours."

"Mine by law, perhaps, though it could never be so in truth. I will not take your money, your only means of support and independence, away from you."

Margaret looked away, hurt and disappointed. Hannah looked at her son. "You should listen to Margaret. You will never find a more willing investor."

"My mind is made up, mother," Thornton replied firmly, though he did observe Margaret's expression with concern. It occurred to him that perhaps he should have spoken to her about this subject in private rather than bring it up for the first time at the breakfast table. Yesterday's events, though delightfully concluded, had proceeded too quickly to permit the level of reflection which he usually brought to business matters.

Margaret sat with downcast eyes, not touching her food, while John looked down the length of the table at her, his forehead beginning to crease. Hannah looked at Margaret with concern, and then glared angrily at her son. Without warning she stood and left the room, her skirts swishing indignantly behind her. Thornton ate his remaining bites of food wolfishly, then glanced at the clock. "Margaret, I have to leave soon. Please do not let us quarrel on the first day of our engagement."

"What is there to quarrel about? Your mind is quite made up." Margaret answered with a false sincerity that her intended did not sense. Had he known her better, had his own emotions not still been so aroused, he would have recognized the concealed emotion in her tone and the masked expression on her face. As it was, he smiled in relief.

"I am glad you understand." He drank the rest of his tea in one gulp and stood, then came to her where she still sat motionless. He placed his hand lightly on her shoulder. "My love, I shall see you again later today." Margaret looked up and gave her bravest smile, in which Thornton saw only what he wanted to see. He swiftly leaned down and kissed her on the cheek, then left the room. Margaret heard his quick step move through the house, collecting his things and bidding his mother farewell, and then the opening and shutting of the front door announced his departure. After a minute Hannah re-entered the room and looked at her sharply.

"What is this nonsense of John's? Were you able to talk him out of it?"

"Not at all. He will not take my money."

"Surely you tried to convince him?"

"There was no time. He had to leave already."

Hannah sat heavily down again at the table. "Thornton men can be pig-headed about money."

Margaret stared at her in shock. In her upbringing, money had rarely been discussed so freely, or with such frankness.

"John is just like his father," Hannah commented, resuming her breakfast. "Oh, I do not mean *that*," she added, seeing Margaret's look of dismay, "I just mean that they are bound and determined to be the only means of support for their family. John handles his money much more responsibly than his father ever did; the mill's failure was not his fault, as I am sure you know. But he and his father share the same trait as most men, I suppose--they will not allow that they might ever be dependent on a woman!"

"But John would *not* be dependent on me, if he were to take my money," Margaret protested. "It is merely an investment, just as any other investment would be. He could pay me back if that were so important to him."

"But you are not any other investor; you will be his wife, and he feels obliged to be *your* provider, not the other way around. It will be hard enough for him to accept that you come to him as an independently wealthy woman, needing nothing from him. He will need time to become accustomed to the idea."

"It is not true that I need nothing from him," said Margaret, vehemently, "but what I do need, I scarcely know how to describe."

Hannah did not seem to hear her. "John's father, now, could have saved himself and the rest of us much trouble, if he had not been so determined to set things right on his own. He had his pride, you see. He would ask no one for either help or counsel, and no matter how badly his affairs went, he refused to admit his troubles even to me. He would be beholden to no one."

"I never imagined that John--Mr. Thornton--would refuse to accept my help," said Margaret, her voice revealing her distress. "I do not want it to be a point of contention between us."

"Talk to him," Hannah urged her, "and tell him how you feel about his refusal. In time he may come to accept your offer in the spirit in which it was made. But do not push too hard. You will have to find your own ways of convincing him to accept your assistance without injuring his pride."

Chapter Four

An Unexpected Setback

"I am flattered, sir, by your consideration of this post. But upon reflection I realize that I do not currently have enough business to consider taking on another manager."

Thornton frowned as he looked at the portly Mr. Slickson sitting across from him, his lips curled thinly together in a half-smile. Mr. Slickson was the master who had asked Thornton for a meeting before Thornton had gone to Havre and Helstone. He was the one who had said he always had room for a talented, thinking man who knew how to make the difficult decisions of business every day; but now that tune had abruptly changed.

"Forgive me--did I misunderstand you previously when you said you might have a position for me?"

"This is business, Thornton. You know how quickly circumstances can change."

"But it was only ten days ago," Thornton began, "No, just a week, that you asked me to call on you!"

"Yes, well, I am sorry for raising expectations that I could not fulfill. At the time I believed I had a position open for a man of vision, for a man who is willing to take risks."

Thornton stiffened. "Do you no longer believe that I am such a man? As a fellow master, you surely recall that is not the case. It was I who took the risk of hiring the Irish to break the strike this past year, nobody else."

"As I have said, circumstances change quickly." Slickson's eyes flickered involuntarily to a small stack of calling cards lodged carelessly against a stack of ledgers and it was then, with his own gaze following Slickson's, that Thornton caught a glimpse of the name Arthur Watson. "As a manager I would expect you to look for chances to expand, to recognize opportunities as they are presented to you, to reach forth and seize the day when those moments come. You no longer strike me as such a man."

Watson was Fanny's husband, the gentleman who had pressed Thornton to take part in a wildly risky speculation that held the possibility of impressive wealth on one hand and utter destruction on the other. Fanny had scorned Thornton when he declined to risk his own welfare, and that of others, on such a needless and greedy venture.

Slickson caught Thornton's eye as it fastened on the calling card and smiled grimly. "Thornton, you know I think the world of your capabilities in general, but in this instance," he nodded at the calling card, "I find myself unable to offer you a position. Perhaps at a later date you might approach me again."

Had Watson taken to blackballing him? Thornton stood abruptly, barely keeping his temper in check. "I quite understand you, sir, and beg your pardon for taking so much of your time. You have made your opinion quite clear. Good day to you." He left the room without bothering to wait for Slickson's reply, his thoughts racing furiously towards his sister and her husband.

Thornton could not imagine Watson bringing pressure to bear against anyone employing his own brother-in-law; it made no sense. Why should he care where Thornton was employed, so long as it was something respectable? They were related now, associated in nearly as close a way as possible, and what lifted the tides of fortune for one would benefit the other as well. Perhaps Watson had been more angered by his refusal to participate than Thornton had thought at first. He strode angrily down the streets of Milton, looking neither to the left or the right, thinking hard and trying to decide what to do next.

As he walked, he reflected again on the speculation as it had been offered to him; he recalled quite clearly the day the whole plan had been laid out, in Watson's office outside Hayleigh Mills. The scheme had been set in South America.

"That infamous revolutionary, Simon Diego, has a grand plan for the re-taking of Venezuela, and if we can give him the assistance he desires, we will be rich beyond our wildest dreams," Watson had assured him, his eyes glistening with greed.

"Does he require that we raise soldiers to march in his army?" Thornton had asked, already wary. Plans based on bloodshed and revolutions were always risky; the winds of war changed without warning.

"No; he requires only financing for his great adventure."

"On what terms? What would be our security?"

"He requires an investment of no less than ten thousand pounds from each of his investors, with which he will purchase arms, ammunition, and other supplies needed for his army. In return, when he has re-taken his country he will provide us with preferential pricing on contracts for cacao, fine lumber, and other commodities, and he will give us an extraordinary interest," here Watson's voice dropped to a hungry whisper, "in silver mines!"

"Silver mines?" Thornton had raised a doubtful eyebrow. "Have you seen these mines for yourself? Have you inspected them at all?"

"I have not, but I have heard them described by those who have. They are known to be in existence, operating as we speak, and their potential has barely been tapped! The constant turmoil in Venezuelan politics makes it difficult to explore and exploit the mines properly; a new tunnel is scarcely dug before the workers must drop their shovels to take up muskets But once Diego comes to power the turmoil will end, Venezuela will enter a new era of prosperity, and we will be richer than we ever imagined!"

"And what if this revolution of Diego's fails?"

"All business is risk, Thornton; I will not deny it. But the man has taken large portions of the country already, and stands to take the rest in one sweep. Renewed, re-supplied, and with the proven support of the common people, he has little risk of failure. As security Diego will forward three large shipments of cacao directly to our agents upon commitment of our funds. Cacao is nearly as good as gold when it is in the right hands! I am telling you, Thornton, we will make a hundred to one on this investment; nay, even a thousand to one when Diego's bold scheme goes forward!"

"I'll not risk it." Thornton's answer had been firm and decisive. "If Diego loses we do too; even if he wins he may be overthrown in his turn, and then what becomes of all your efforts?"

"Ten thousand pounds is a fortune, I admit. But great rewards come to those who take great risks." Watson eyed him closely, waiting for his answer.

Thornton shook his head. "My mind's made up, Watson; I'll not invest in your scheme."

Only a few months later, the papers had been full of the news of Diego's burgeoning success. The revolution was marching steadily across Venezuela, and Diego had taken his victory. Profitable contracts had already improved the fortunes of those who had invested. Yet Thornton, even now, did not regret his decision. All business might be speculation, but he would never risk his entire business and be unable to meet payroll for his workers if it failed. Nor would he risk funds invested with him by others; his reputation was his most valuable asset.

The thought of investors brought Margaret to mind, and he smiled to himself. *Her* investment offer had been a token, a means of communicating the change in her affections for him; after all, a woman could hardly approach a man she had once spurned and simply announce that she had changed her mind about him. Thornton had, in all honesty, scarcely been listening to her words at the time. He had been more absorbed in reading the lines of Margaret's face, and regretting his own cold behavior towards her. But the few words he did comprehend had given him sudden hope, and his immediate, almost involuntary response had been to take her hand in his, with delightful results.

And now they were to be married. It went sorely against the grain that he would not be able to offer Margaret everything he could have offered her when he was a master. She deserved better than to marry a man lately come down in the world, a man who used to employ hundreds and now would be dependent on others for his living. But taking Margaret's inheritance and using it for his own schemes would be the ultimate admission of his inability to provide for her. He would not do it; his entire soul shrank from the idea. He would make certain to see to her needs, instead, by insisting that her money be settled on her in the most secure way possible, and by ensuring that she would be provided for even after his death. He was glad that Margaret had understood his view on this subject so readily, and given up the idea so easily--another example of her fine and gracious personality.

He could not go home yet. To return home so quickly would be an admission of failure to those he loved most, and he would cause them no anxiety. Instead he would spend the rest of the day leaving his card with other gentlemen of his acquaintance, determined to find the one door that would open new opportunities to him, so that he could begin again his slow climb back to the status he had once enjoyed. He would end his day by calling on Arthur Watson himself and determining what manner of objection the man had against him, and how he might best react to this newest setback.

Chapter Five

The Woman You Wish To Marry

There was little about John Thornton's appearance that Margaret had not learned to know almost as well as she knew her own. Every small detail of his form and dress, the way he carried himself, and the varied expressions on his face had long ago been observed, unconsciously committed to memory, and treasured in her heart. She had grown to admire his tall form and broad shoulders when he stood at his most upright, and the way his hair turned from ebony black to a dark auburn when he walked in full sunlight. She thrilled to hear the deep timbre of his voice whenever he said her name in his tender way, and she understood every shadow of expression that crossed his face, whether happy or uneasy, even if she did not always comprehend what stirred those emotions.

So it was that when Thornton returned to the house at the end of his long day and she watched through the curtains to see him ascend the steps, she understood by the slight frown on his face and his slowed movements that his business had not gone well. But when he entered the house and handed off his coat and hat, his eyes met Margaret's, and the deeper creases on his forehead disappeared. His smile softened the angular lines of his face, and she saw that just being in her presence was enough to make his troubles momentarily lighter. When they had a moment of privacy he came and took her in his arms, and the feeling of the comfort she could give him was a heavenly taste of the delights that would be theirs daily once the wedding took place. She instantly resolved to do nothing that would cause his troubled look to return that day; she would say nothing, yet, of her hurt at his curt dismissal that morning of her assistance in his business. Instead she set herself to helping the maid prepare his tea and setting a welcome place for him in the sitting room to enjoy it.

It was not until supper that Thornton began to ask about the day his mother and his beloved had spent together, and to inquire about their plans for the wedding. Margaret would much rather hear about his day, but she answered his questions gladly and in a way that left him in no doubt of her eagerness to be married.

"Two weeks gives us precious little time for proper wedding attire, but Margaret is not difficult to satisfy, and I believe we will, between the two of us, contrive something that is more than respectable," said Hannah in her proud way. Thornton looked at Margaret appraisingly.

"Why not wear what you have on now? It is quite lovely to me," he said, with innocent seriousness.

"This is a plain calico; it would not possibly serve!" Margaret protested, beginning to laugh. "Imagine you, a draper's assistant, being ignorant of women's fashions!"

"I cannot deny the charge," Thornton concurred with a slight smile. "We men are practical creatures and see little need for all the notions, flowers, bonnets, and everything else which women consider as necessary to a wedding as the minister himself."

"And that is why women arrange these things, and men merely observe them," Margaret answered, relieved to see his good cheer.

"And pay for them," Thornton added good-naturedly, to smiles all around.

"Fanny was quite amazed to see Miss Hale with me today. She said to give you her congratulations, despite her disappointment that she will not be the center of attention for the next few weeks, at least," Hannah said.

"I am glad of it," Thornton replied shortly.

"It is certainly convenient that she was married so recently," Hannah continued. "My experience with her wedding will make it much easier to order the flowers, food and everything else for yours."

"The food, mother?" Thornton looked puzzled.

"For the wedding breakfast, of course. Have you forgotten so quickly that a wedding breakfast is customary after the ceremony?"

"I must admit that it had slipped my mind."

"It will not be a large breakfast, of course," Margaret assured him. "I hope to hear soon that my cousin and her husband will be here for the occasion. Besides them and Higgins, my side of the church will be quite empty."

"There will be a fair number of masters there," Hannah reminded her. "And my friends will be happy to welcome you into our family, and into Milton society."

Thornton said nothing, for this second mention of masters had turned his mind back to his interview with Watson, concluded not long before he had returned home that afternoon. Watson had not been encouraging towards his efforts to re-establish himself in trade.

"How can I help you, Thornton?" Watson had asked after the customary salutations had been exchanged. They were back in Watson's office, the same place where Watson's original offer had been made, overlooking the great floor of Watson's own mill. The smell of calico and dye permeated the air, making it difficult to speak without choking, but Thornton met his eyes evenly.

"Are you blackballing me, Watson?" he demanded. "That is what I came here to ask."

"Blackballing you!" Watson's eyes opened wide. "What do you mean by blackballing?"

"Watson, you know I need work. Slickson as much as offered me a position less than a fortnight ago, before I had to travel on business, but when I saw him this morning the offer was withdrawn. His manner of speaking made me think that you might have something to do with it."

"I? I think not! You are my wife's brother; why wouldn't I want you to prosper? I wish you nothing but success in your future endeavors."

Thornton's eyes narrowed as he looked at him. "Then you've no idea of turning people away from hiring me?"

"Of course not. The masters have come to their own conclusions about your suitability for hire." Though the words were polite, Watson's voice had suddenly become wry, and Thornton studied him more closely.

"I don't think I like your tone, Watson."

"What's my tone to do with anything? You were offered a perfectly respectable business opportunity and you chose not to take advantage of it. Nobody needs my recommendation to see your failings for himself. When others ask my opinion, I give it. You can ask no more of me than that."

"I can ask for a little loyalty, by God!"

"Shall I tell others to hire a man I would not have? Is that who you think me to be, Thornton? I have threatened no man; I have given no character for you, whether good or ill. All I have done is to tell others who asked that my wife's own brother did not think enough of me to throw his fortune in with mine, and that consequently I had to risk much more of my own capital--happily, as it turned out. And now he comes with hat in hand, looking for work as a manager! You had best set your sights lower, Thornton; perhaps someone somewhere will take you on as a clerk." With that, Watson had pointedly taken up the daily paper to read, with an article about the ongoing revolution in Venezuela prominently displayed in order to make his point. Thornton had stared at him for a long moment, and then left the room in anger. He knew that Watson had taken offense for his not joining in the venture, but had not suspected it had gone this far.

"John, did you hear me?" his mother's voice broke in, and Thornton realized he had been lost in his own thoughts. "I asked if your meeting this morning was a success."

"I can manage my own affairs, mother," he answered irritably. Both women looked at him, and he added, with a tinge of remorse, "I apologize; my business did not end as I wished it to, but you need not worry. It will be resolved soon enough." The two women exchanged a look but said nothing further.

The subject was dropped until after supper, when the three sat together in the parlor. Thornton and Margaret sat together on the high-backed settee in front of the fireplace, though no fire was lit this evening. Hannah chose to sit as far from the young couple as she reasonably could while still being in the same room, and she gave a fair imitation of being absolutely oblivious to their presence from her chair in the corner of the room. Their season of courtship would be brief, and she felt they deserved every bit of pleasure from it that she could reasonably give them. Therefore she called her maid to attend to her while she sewed, carried on a lively conversation with her so as to mask the other conversation taking place, and scarcely looked in their direction at all.

Margaret was now hoping for an opportunity to ask Thornton about his business of the morning, and Thornton, despite his delight at being with Margaret, could not help replaying his interview with Watson over again in his mind. It was therefore perhaps inevitable that the subject which had been so carefully avoided would begin to spring forth when Thornton said, with her hand in his, "I am so thankful that you have chosen to accept me despite my business failure. I know I have very little to offer you in material goods."

"I do not agree with your assessment of yourself," Margaret answered, anxious to reassure him. "You have been humbled a little, perhaps, by the closing of the mill, but you are still in essentials all that you were previously."

"You do not understand." Thornton smiled sadly. "It is possible, love, that you will marry neither a master nor a manager, but only a humble clerk."

"A clerk? Your interview this morning was for a manager's position."

"Yes, but," he hesitated, "it did not go as planned. That is why I stayed out of the house so long today. I found that I may have to move quite far down in the world before I can ever move back up."

Margaret pressed affectionately on his arm. "I wish you would tell me everything that happened today. If we are to be married, it is only right that I know what is troubling you."

Thornton's pride fought against this for a moment, but the prospect of sharing his burden with the woman he loved prevailed, and he was able to tell Margaret every detail of Slickson's refusal and Watson's anger. Poor Margaret! She felt a helpless anger growing as he spoke and a burning desire to avenge the wrongs being carried out against him, but at the same time she was glad that he had been able to share his worries with her. There was sweetness in knowing she could offer him some small relief.

"And so I do not know where or if I shall find any useful employment at all, Margaret," Thornton finished in frustration. "I can only hope that this does not delay our wedding."

"I do not believe that it will," she responded stoutly. "Watson's word will not outweigh the entire community; other men already know your character."

"I hope that they do, but we must prepare ourselves for the worst. It may take some time to find work, and I cannot marry you until I have some hope of supporting you."

Margaret caught her breath in dismay. "You will not marry me until you find employment?"

"I cannot see my way clear to it." Thornton's face showed his own disappointment at such an outcome. "A man should be able to support his family."

Margaret chose her words carefully. "But if you will use my money to invest in the mill, we will support each other. As I told you before, all that I have will be yours on our wedding day."

"I thought we resolved this issue this morning, Margaret." Thornton frowned as he looked at his intended. "I told you then that I will never use your money as my own. What sort of man relies on his wife's inheritance, stealing away what is meant to secure her future, instead of adding to it with his own earnings? I am not that man, Margaret. Do not ask it of me." Neither noticed that Hannah had dismissed the maid; she was listening as well as she could without being obvious.

"I might just as well ask, then, what sort of man refuses to accept his wife as a full partner in their marriage?" Margaret asked, unable to restrain herself any longer. "God has granted me a fortune to dispose of as I wish, and if I choose by my own mind to use it to forward our marriage by removing any impediments in our way, it is no reflection upon you!"

"You will be more than my partner," rejoined Thornton, his voice beginning to rise in frustration. For the first time he remembered his mother's presence, glancing furtively at her while she pretended great dedication to her stitching. He moved closer to Margaret and spoke more quietly. "You will be--you are--my superior in every way. You are my angel, above and beyond the best possible part of me. You will bring so much to me that I can never hope to equal or repay."

"But I am not your partner if I am not allowed to join in all your trials and successes!" Margaret would not accept his diversion. "You would have me stay separate from them, able to look on but never able to take full part by lending you my assistance. Your view of me as your superior is a barrier you must overcome. It keeps me from you as surely as my former prejudices against you did."

"I would not say that it keeps me from you. We are engaged to be married, are we not? Have we not come together despite our differences?"

"Together and yet not together, if you say we cannot marry until you find employment. Use my money, John, and start the mill again, and then all the rest of this goes away."

"It would be a stain on my honor," he insisted stubbornly, unwilling to yield the point.

"Your honor is no friend to me!" Margaret pulled her hand from his. Before he could entirely comprehend what had happened, she stood and swept out the door, retreating to some unknown part of the house. He rose to go after her, but Hannah likewise stood and blocked his way from the room. He was amazed to see a knowing smile on her face.

"Now I see what has drawn you to Margaret so much for all these months."

"I must follow her; please step aside!"

"I will not until you have listened to me for a minute, John Thornton. Margaret is absolutely right. You should take her money and open the mill again, and be glad for the good fortune God has brought to you instead of being so stubbornly set on having everything your own way."

"Mother--you would take her side against me?"

"Margaret is your equal in every way. I had my doubts before, but there is no question in my mind now. She will not yield to you when your pride makes you foolish, and she has the courage to stand up to you when you are wrong. She will be a splendid wife for you."

"You need not tell me that, Mother. I have wanted to be her husband for many months now. But there are certain things about me she will need to understand first."

Hannah nearly laughed outright. "She understands you better than you understand yourself. It is you who must come to know the character of the woman you wish to marry!"

"I love her! How can you say I do not know her?"

"I did not say you do not know her at all, but you have a great deal yet to understand about her character. You are not marrying a wallflower, a pretty ornament who will sit quietly at your side and agree with whatever you say. She has a mind of her own, and the will to throw herself fully into any endeavor she chooses."

"I know all that! It is what drew me to her."

"And yet you resist it now. You insist that she sit meekly by while you strive and fight, instead of allowing her to join you fully! You demand that she not offend your pride while you forget the pride she overcame to give you her affections. Do not let that pride separate you now. Accept what she wants to give you, and thank Providence for bringing such a woman into your life. You will not regret it."

Thornton was silent for a moment, absorbing her words. "I will think on what you say, Mother. But allow me to go to her now, I beg of you."

Hannah stepped aside as Thornton brushed past her, a small smile still playing on her lips. "Engaged for only a day, and already their first disagreement!" she thought to herself. "Margaret Hale will be either the making or the breaking of you, John Thornton!"

Chapter Six

Negotiations

Thornton found Margaret standing in the kitchen, her arms uncharacteristically folded over her chest, staring out the small window into the dark of the evening outside. Two small lamps lit the room from their stations on the dry sink and on the small table usually reserved only for servants. Although Margaret must have guessed his presence by the sound of his footsteps, she did not turn or acknowledge his presence in any way.

Thornton looked at her helplessly for a moment, wondering what to say in order to heal the sudden breach between them. Unbidden, the first words that came to his mind came out of their own accord. "Margaret, I love you."

"And I love you," she answered at once, although Thornton could tell by the long, shuddering breath she took that the words had come with an effort. Relief surged through him. He stepped closer, placing his hand on her elbow.

"Then come and sit at the table with me, and let us resolve this," he urged. "I dislike having anything between us."

Margaret slowly turned to face him and looked up at him for a long moment, and Thornton caught his breath at the beauty of her face as the lamplight reflected off of it and in her eyes. All thought of sitting fled. He drew her instead into his arms, and felt her sigh as she relaxed into his embrace, letting her head rest on his shoulder. He savored the moment in silence and for long moments neither one moved. Then Thornton said, "Put your arms around my neck the way you did on the day of the riot, my love."

Margaret must have had the same thought, for her hands were already moving before he had finished speaking. With her form completely encased in his arms, Thornton leaned down to kiss her again the way he had on the train platform, and Margaret accepted his attentions eagerly. After a minute, Thornton broke off to gaze tenderly at her.

"I am sorry, my love, that I did not understand how important this is to you. I thought we had ended the argument when I left the house this morning."

"What was there to argue about?" Margaret answered, using the same words she had said to him in the morning. "Your mind was quite made up." Despite her words, she let her head rest against his chest again, making the delightful discovery that she could hear his heart beating from that position. The steady rhythm against her cheek soothed her more than she could have thought possible.

"I have a great deal to learn," Thornton admitted, enjoying every sensation of the moment as he held her close. "I beg of you to be patient, love. I am accustomed to giving orders to my men, not to making decisions with another person. I suppose my first lesson will be to remember that your silence is not always your agreement."

"And I will also need to learn to accommodate your views," Margaret responded. "Neither of us may run roughshod over the other's feelings. I *do* understand that being able to support me is important to you, John."

Relief surged through Thornton. "I think perhaps a compromise is needed," he said. Reluctantly, he separated from Margaret and pulled out one of the kitchen chairs for her, then sat in another chair, pulling it as close to her as humanly possible. Although he had already skirted the rules of propriety enough for one night, he could not resist holding one of her hands in his again as he looked at her intently.

"May I make you a promise, Margaret? If you are in agreement I will continue to look for a position, but nothing will be allowed to interfere with our wedding in two weeks. Our marriage will go forward and if necessary, we will use your money to support us until an acceptable way for me to support you can be found. Will that be enough to satisfy you?"

Margaret had hoped for more, but she resolved to press carefully. "What about my investment in your mill? Will you allow it now?"

"I will consider it, especially if I can also find a way to guarantee your financial security," John replied, regarding her seriously, and Margaret decided she would have to be satisfied for the moment.

"Very well. I accept your compromise, if we may re-visit this issue from time to time."

Thornton smiled. "My love, you are relentless. I should have asked you to deal with my striking workers. You bargain well."

"We are on the same side of this disagreement, John. We just need to learn to listen to each other more before we become angry."

"I shall look forward to learning that lesson again every day," said Thornton, and their first disagreement ended with an affectionate kiss.

Chapter Seven

Planning

After this nothing more was said about Margaret's money for several days. They were blissful days, full of happy anticipation and busy planning. Margaret and Hannah had taken on the responsibility of cleaning and organizing the house, moving Hannah out of the master bedroom and placing Thornton's things there instead. The room next to it, destined for Margaret, had been aired and was now being thoroughly cleaned. New bedding and other furnishings were chosen and ordered. Besides all this, the women were working steadily on the wedding dress and other clothes, and so the days sped by.

Although Margaret and Thornton discussed several plans for a wedding trip, in the end they settled on a simple itinerary. The newlyweds would proceed directly from the church to the Outwood station, there to take a train to Bath, where they would stay for a week. On their return they would stop in London for three days to visit with Edith and the captain, assuming her cousin agreed to such a plan. Margaret was still waiting for a letter from Edith congratulating her on her engagement to Thornton. The addition of such a visit at the end of their wedding trip was all that was needed to make it perfect in Margaret's eyes and she looked forward to quickly settling this detail with her cousin.

Thornton continued to look for work among the masters of Milton. He quickly found that this group could be divided fairly evenly into two camps. The first camp consisted of those masters who had thrown their lot in with Watson, and amongst them he received a tepid welcome. None spoke as bluntly as Slickson had, but they all made it clear that his lack of participation in the speculation had damaged him materially in their eyes. They expressed great sympathy for him and a certain amount of admiration for his past leadership, but none would acknowledge that they could use his talent in their own enterprise.

The second group was made of masters who had not joined with Watson, either because they had not been asked or because they too had experienced reservations against such a risky scheme. This group was warmly enthusiastic upon hearing from Thornton, but none of them had an open position. Thornton's mill had not been the only one to shut down and there were several other masters who had suffered some of the same setbacks Thornton had experienced after the strike. Work was hard to come by. But they all said they would call on him as soon as a position became available.

Thornton was thinking of all these things as he walked home at the end of the day. Despite his disappointment regarding work, he stepped energetically, eager to share the results of his final errand of the day with Margaret. He had called on the local parson and obtained a marriage license, now safe in his coat pocket, and one more barrier to their union was out of the way.

A young boy with fair hair, known to him by sight as the son of one of his former employees named Mason, came out of a side street as he approached, attempting to press the daily paper into Thornton's hand. Something about the boy's gaunt face struck him and although he was eager to be home, Thornton paused to buy a paper, more out of sympathy for the child than from a desire to read any news. As he searched in his pocket for change, he could not help wondering where the lad's father was working now.

"Your father--which mill did he go to? Has he made any advances since he worked for me?" he asked, tossing him a coin. The boy caught it eagerly.

"He hasn't had any work. None of the masters is hiring right now."

"Has he been out of work this whole time? How is he supporting you?"

"My sisters hired themselves out for maids, and my mother takes in laundry whenever she can get someone to pay."

"And you sell papers," Thornton finished, eyeing the lad more carefully, surmising that the incomes described did not adequately support the family. The child's clothes fit, but just barely, and there were holes in the thin patches that covered the elbows of his jacket. "What is your name?"

"James."

"And what have you eaten today, James?"

"'Tweren't nothing in the house this morning, sir."

Thornton withdrew more coins and pressed them into James' hand, watching his eyes grow wide with delight. "Thank you, sir!"

"Make sure to look for me tomorrow, and I will buy a paper from you every day."

"You can count on me! Thank you, sir!" James smiled widely and turned quickly, clutching his fist full of coins tightly. Thornton stood for a moment, watching him thoughtfully as he hurried away; then called out to his retreating back.

"James!"

James stopped in his headlong rush, looking back at Thornton with a puzzled expression.

"Save your coins, lad, and come with me. I'll not send you home on an empty stomach."

So it was that Margaret, who was watching out the window for Thornton's return, was surprised to see him accompanied by a slender, serious looking boy of about ten years, who entered the house silently and stood in the entry with wide-eyed wonder. He was so overwhelmed by his surroundings that he forgot to express his gratitude after Thornton had given directions to have him shown into the kitchen and given a substantial meal. Margaret gazed after him in her gentle, inquiring way, and Thornton explained how he had come to bring him home.

"It was kind of you to think of his needs," said Margaret, after hearing the story. "I will see that he is given a basket to take home as well."

"I would appreciate any help you can give them," Thornton answered. "Mason worked for me for years; it pains me to see his reduced circumstances." Margaret assured him that she would do everything she could for the family, and then asked if he had met with any success that day in his search for a position.

"I have not," said Thornton, "but I did accomplish one thing that will please you, I hope," and he withdrew the marriage license he had obtained and displayed it proudly. Margaret smiled as she took in the significance of the paper in his hand. Thornton could not resist teasing her.

"You know, with this license there is nothing to stop us from marrying right away. We could be wed tomorrow morning if you wish, and if you think your clothes are already adequate."

Margaret recognized his humor. "With all the work your mother has put into them, I doubt very much if she would appreciate such an abrupt change in plans. We will have to be patient a little while longer."

Thornton moved towards her then, but stopped as a servant entered the room, and Margaret saw the annoyance on his face from the inability to embrace her as he wished. "I hope the nine days pass very quickly indeed, my love," he said instead, and Margaret had no doubt from the look on his face that he meant it.

It was not until after tea that Thornton remembered the paper he had bought and decided to make use of it. While Margaret and his mother helped the maid clear the cups and plates, he brought the paper out and opened it, flipping through its pages in his customary way, looking for any items that might be of interest for business men or that might particularly impact the town of Milton. An item several pages in caught his attention, and as he read more, he leaned forward with heightened interest. As he read it again the lines on his forehead deepened.

"You look quite fierce, John," Hannah commented, as she and Margaret entered the room again, their arms full of candles to be trimmed. "What has your attention?"

"It is an item which will be of interest to many here in Milton," Thornton replied, running his hand worriedly along his chin. "It seems that Watson's investment in South America might not be as lucrative as he first thought. It may in fact be quite in danger."

"In South America!" Hannah, who had never asked for the particulars of Watson's speculation, exclaimed. "What has Watson to do with South America?"

Thornton explained the details of Watson's plan. He did not need to describe the reasons for his own reservations against such a scheme; Hannah, who had known so much financial hardship in her own life, was never inclined to risk money needlessly.

"I completely understand your hesitation now," she said with satisfaction, while Margaret listened gravely. "If I had known about Watson's scheme myself, I would have advised Fanny to argue strenuously against it! Men have lost fortunes on ventures not half as risky. Money is not made or kept by gambling on every change of fortune."

"What does the newspaper say about the speculation?" Margaret asked.

"Nothing in particular; the news is of Diego himself. It seems his revolution has not gone smoothly of late, and our observers report to

London that his new government is in grave danger of falling. The rebels are within reach of the capital. It may have fallen already; this news is at least two weeks old and with such a delay in reporting it is hard to know."

"If he has fallen, then the masters here will have little hope of the contracts they bargained for," Hannah observed. "Their plans will have come to nothing."

"And there will be no chance of gain from the silver mines, either, which was their greater goal," Thornton agreed.

"But the principal that the masters invested--will they lose that as well?" Margaret asked, concerned. Thornton considered the question briefly before responding.

"The investors have already gained back most of what they advanced in the form of the cacao beans which Diego sent as security, but some would still be at risk. It was mostly used to purchase the arms and other weapons used by Diego's men. If Diego conducts an orderly retreat and brings his arms with him, all may still be well. He can regroup with his men at a distance and conduct a new campaign, if possible, to regain his capital city. But if Diego falls, then all the money Watson counted on receiving will be gone as quickly as it came."

"And the effect on Watson and the others?" his mother inquired.

Thornton shook his head worriedly, his hand still stroking his chin. "That is a question which only Watson can answer."

Chapter Eight

Interruptions

Fanny arrived the next morning as soon as polite social calls could be made, her eyes flashing angrily as soon as she stepped in the door of the parlor and saw her brother. She completely skipped over any pleasant formalities to start her visit. "I hope you know that this is all your fault, John. Watson would not be nearly so exposed to danger if you had just taken your part in the venture as he asked. He was quite distraught last night."

"And a good morning to you too, Fanny. I am as happy to see you as you are to see me," John responded, his eyes flashing in return. He noted that Fanny took it for granted that he was aware of her husband's financial danger.

Fanny tossed her head and sniffed resentfully. "You needn't be so indignant with me, John! It was your duty to support your brother, my husband, and you turned him down!"

"You are not endearing yourself to me at this moment, Fanny, by presuming that I should ever have followed your business advice."

"But if you had thrown your lot in with him and the other masters, the risk would not have been as great! They were forced to raise more money amongst themselves to make up for what you would not put forward, and now they are doubly exposed."

"That is not *my* fault," Thornton answered, his voice beginning to rise, but Hannah stepped between the two.

"That is enough! Fanny Watson, you should be ashamed of yourself," she interposed, putting an end to the discussion. "Your husband urged your brother to take part in a wild, unreliable speculation, and John, being the honorable man that he is, turned it down. It was his choice to make as he wished-- and I for one am glad he did not give in! You have no business coming here to rail on him simply because your husband may be regretting his own foolishness."

Fanny, flushed and unhappy, glared back at both of them but dared not say a word in response to her mother. She did not notice as Margaret stepped closer and she flinched when a gentle hand was placed on her arm.

"Please sit down, Mrs. Watson," said Margaret comfortingly. "Did you walk all the way here, in this heat? I hope you will rest a little while before leaving again."

Fanny seemed to recover herself somewhat at the conciliatory gesture. She fluttered her fan and held her head a little higher, though her voice softened slightly. "I actually came to see you, not to rail on John, as mother puts it. I did not even expect to see him here. I thought he would be busy at whatever work he has now."

"I have no work, thanks to your husband. I stayed home today in order to tend to correspondence," Thornton replied evenly, folding his arms over his chest as he gazed, unblinking, at his sister. Fanny's face reddened even more, but Margaret intervened before she could respond.

"Come with me and let me get you some tea," she said hastily, drawing Fanny away; and so further argument between brother and sister was avoided, though tension remained in each face.

When all were seated comfortably and the tea had been poured Fanny spoke to Margaret. "I came here today to offer my help to you, Miss Hale." At Margaret's look of inquiry she continued. "I know that you are marrying John at the end of next week, and it is simply not possible to have a proper wedding dress constructed in such a short time. One may sew a dress of *some* sort, I suppose, but I know how many yards of lace went into my dress and how long it took to make, and I am certain it will be beyond your capabilities to make a dress anything like it in less than two weeks."

"Your dress was quite lovely; I remember it well," Margaret answered quietly.

"And I thought that, since you and I are of a similar size, you might perhaps like to borrow mine. It will be much easier to take in or let out in a few places, if that is needed, than to sew an entire gown from scratch!"

Margaret paused before she answered, studying the other woman's face carefully. Fanny's offer was generous, but she suspected there was some ulterior motive at play. "I am sure that it would be much easier. You are very kind, Mrs. Watson, but I believe the dress I am working on now will suit admirably. It is more fitting for me, since it is much plainer than yours, and as we will be leaving on the train directly from the ceremony, I think it more appropriate. But I do appreciate your consideration in making the offer."

Fanny was offended. She had never understood this strange Miss Hale from the south, who carried herself with so much poise and grace and yet had barely a penny to her name. She was making a generous offer to this relative stranger and expected to be well rewarded with fawning, slavish gratitude. Nothing of Margaret's change in circumstances had reached her ears, or if it had, she had been too self-absorbed to pay attention to it.

"You need not put on your fine airs and graces with me, Miss Hale! You are the daughter of a poor clergyman who left the church and became nothing but a tutor, and a dress such as mine would ordinarily be quite beyond your means. But I mean to offer it to you anyway, unless you think it beneath you. Really, I don't see why my mother has not proposed such a scheme before now. The dress is yours if you want it, and you ought to be appreciative of the sacrifices others are willing to make on your behalf!"

"You go too far, Fanny," John interjected, his voice stern. "You do not know of what you speak. Margaret needs nothing of yours."

"Indeed, she is quite an heiress," Hannah added, her own voice angry. "I am surprised you didn't hear of her good fortune before now. Miss Hale's godfather was Mr. Bell, who owned Marlborough Mills and a good number of other properties in Milton, and Mr. Bell has passed all his property on to Margaret. So you see, Fanny, Miss Hale is wealthier than we are now. She owns the very home we are in right now! If anyone has been putting on airs and graces, it is you."

Poor Fanny hardly knew where to look after this pronouncement. Her eyes grew wide as she looked back and forth between the three others, and for a moment she appeared to gasp for breath. But when the moment had passed she did a tolerable job of pulling herself up with as much dignity as possible, wrapping her injured pride around her like a blanket, her chin held higher than ever. "I wish you had told me this before," she finally said. "You might have mentioned it before I went and made myself ridiculous."

Margaret had had enough. "Come, Mrs. Watson, to blame anyone is useless. I would not have us quarrel when we are going to be sisters so soon. I thank you for your kind offer of the use of your dress on my wedding day, but I can assure you that it is not necessary. My own dress will be complete in plenty of time for the ceremony. Thanks to your mother it is almost ready now. But please do accept my deepest gratitude for your thoughtfulness and consideration, and my hopes that in the future we will come to know each other much better than we do now."

It was a valiant attempt on Margaret's part, but the proffered olive branch was not taken, overlooked as it was by Fanny's offended pride. She set her teacup on the table more firmly than it deserved. "Well I'm glad that John, at least, will be marrying someone with money. I'm sure we will all be very grateful to you for keeping a roof over our heads and food on our plates when the time comes! And now, if you'll excuse me, I really must be going."

Thornton sighed in exasperation. "Fanny, it wasn't meant that way! Stay and let us talk this through."

Fanny would have none of it. "My mind is quite made up; Watson is expecting me at home," she said resentfully, seeming more angry than the occasion would allow. Nothing the others could say would stop her; without a look to the left or the right she stood and made her exit, giving the servant barely the opportunity to open the door ahead of her. As she sailed out of the room in a veritable sea of lace and petticoats, Margaret looked after her in concern, while Hannah lifted her chin, clamped her lips together, and resolved to deal with her daughter more firmly in the future regarding her indifference to the feelings of others. Thornton said nothing, but he looked deeply troubled.

"You need not be angry, John, on my behalf," Margaret told him, seeing the look on his face. "I am certain that Fanny is speaking out of fear and for not knowing what may happen to her husband and herself. She does not mean to be hurtful."

"You are right; she does not," Thornton answered. "But she must be worried, herself, to say what she did to me. She has no interest in business; usually she cannot see past the ribbons on her own bonnet to see anything in the paper. I wonder what put it into her head."

"Surely it is not so unusual for a wife to take an avid interest in her husband's concerns? She would not be the first bride to learn a great deal about business from her new husband."

"That only shows how little you know of Fanny," Thornton answered her, with a wry smile.

"John is right," said Hannah decisively. "Fanny Thornton never had one moment of concern about business before now. She was too young when my husband died for it to have had a lasting impact on her. Her memory of our hard years is faint and what she does recall, she pays no mind to. She would rather order an entire wardrobe of new dresses for her wedding than practice a little economy for her brother's sake. The only time I ever saw her interested in any business matter was when she thought they would make a fortune from Watson's scheme!"

"Something tells me that there is more to this speculation than meets the eye," Thornton said, his hand absentmindedly rubbing his chin. "What did she mean by keeping a roof overhead and food on the table?"

"I cannot imagine; surely the venture could not be as bad as all that!" his mother answered, looking doubtful. "You said the investors have already made back most of what they first sank into it."

"I wonder if that is entirely true," Thornton replied, and for some time he stared thoughtfully at nothing in particular, his forehead furrowed deeply as he pondered what, exactly, might be the meaning of his sister's strange words.

Chapter Nine

A Bargain Struck

Although Thornton made various inquiries over the next day to find out more details on the state of Watson's speculation, he was not able to determine any new information. Whatever secrets Watson was hiding, if secrets there were, remained his and his alone. After a day of intense curiosity he resolved to let the matter rest and turn to concerns that were, for him, much more pressing.

"I have come to steal my wife away for a little while, Mother," Thornton announced, coming into the room where Margaret and his mother were working on the afternoon two days after Fanny's visit. "I would like to take her for a walk."

"She is not your wife yet," Hannah said mildly, the corners of her mouth rising slightly.

"No, but she will be soon, and I find I would like to spend some time alone with her--if she is agreeable, that is." Thornton looked at Margaret expectantly, wondering how she would respond to such a direct approach. But Margaret only flushed becomingly as she smiled and set aside her sewing.

"I am certainly agreeable. I have hardly had a chance to walk outdoors at all since returning to Milton."

"Then let us go now. We can go to the park and be back in time for tea."

While Margaret retrieved her hat and light coat, the maid entered the room and handed the day's post to Hannah, who pursed her lips as she glanced through the small assortment. "Here is a letter for Margaret, from London," she said, handing it to her son.

"I will see that she gets it. You do not mind me taking her from you for a short time, do you? We have not had anything like a proper courtship."

"Object? Of course not. It must be difficult to court properly when you are living under the same roof, subject to all the rules of propriety. Take her, keep her safe, and be home in time for tea. In a very little while your separation will be over, completely over, when you are married. Keep that in mind when you are together and exercise patience just a little longer."

"I will. Thank you, Mother." Thornton leaned down to kiss her cheek, and then Hannah heard his footsteps as he moved into the entry way to join Margaret. She sighed heavily as she heard the two young people leave the house.

Margaret was rising higher in Hannah's esteem every day. Were it only for Margaret's love for Thornton, and for Thornton's obvious affection for her, Hannah would have made every effort to welcome her for John's sake. But since she had recently spent so much time with Margaret, Hannah had come to feel a real affection for Margaret herself: for her patience, even temper and high character, and for the realization of how much she would bring to her son's life. She was only too glad to see the new contentment in Thornton's face whenever he looked at his future wife, only too relieved that her son would have someone to care for him as much as he deserved.

Still, the old patterns of life were changing. Fanny was married and would return to the house no more, and John and Margaret would be first in each other's affections from now on. Eventually the children would come, and then she, Hannah, would have an even lower place in her children's priorities. But that was as it should be, and Hannah smiled with bittersweet satisfaction as she stitched new initials into the hand towels.

Outside the house, Thornton took Margaret's arm protectively within his own, holding her closer than strictly necessary as they navigated the crowded streets of Milton. The noises of passersby, delivery carts, and other sounds made any sort of conversation difficult. He let his eyes speak for him instead as he glanced down at her from time to time, while he carefully guided her steps towards one of the parks he had seen her frequent. It would be quieter there, and they would have time and privacy to speak as freely as desired.

Margaret had willingly tucked her hand into his as it rested on his arm. She felt all the delight of walking so closely with the man she loved, his protection around her like a mantle, knowing the thrill of being chosen and adored by the gentleman she respected and admired above all others. It was beautiful, this knowledge of their mutual affection, and the knowledge that they would never need to be separated from each other again. She could still hardly believe the good fortune that had finally brought them together.

Their steps slowed when they entered the park, and Thornton allowed Margaret to pull away from him just enough so that he could more easily see her face. His first sentence was not what she expected at all.

"I think I have never had such a dislike for women's fashions as I do at this moment."

"And what is your objection to women's fashions now? Do you think I ought to wear this dress for our wedding?" she asked laughingly, glancing down.

"No; it is because your hat makes it so inconvenient for me to see your face. How many times in the past did I silently curse it when I encountered you out somewhere, and could not see your every expression! When I saw you at the exhibition in London you did not oblige me by looking up, and so I had to guess at what you were thinking and feeling. If only lady's hats did not have such wide brims."

"I will not take my hat off here in public, but I will make sure to look at you often enough that you will have no doubt of my feelings at any time. Will that do?"

"It will have to, for now. I can hardly wait for the day when there will be no more barriers between us."

Margaret flushed and looked away, but Thornton sensed her pleasure in his comment by the small smile that played on her lips. He continued, "I have neglected you, I fear. I have been so preoccupied with trying to get myself established in business again that I have not spent as much time with you as I ought. This season of courtship will be brief, and I ought to make the most of it."

"I have missed you sometimes, but I understand your preoccupation," Margaret answered honestly. "As you say, it is only for a short time, and I have used the time to come to know your mother better."

"And how do you get on with my mother? Are you friends?"

"We are beginning to be. She seems to have accepted me completely, and I am grateful. It would be difficult if we did not get along well together."

"I am glad to hear it." They walked on in silence together before Margaret asked her own question.

"When we met again on the train platform you could not have known I would be there at that time. How did you come to be there at the same time?"

"Higgins had told me about your brother before I went to Havre, and I stopped in Helstone on my way back so that I might in some way feel closer to you. I was compelled to walk the same steps you had taken, breathe the same air you breathed, and touch the same places you had touched, and wonder if you could ever forgive me for doubting you. I determined to return to Milton and work out some way of approaching you again, if I could gain the courage. When I saw you there on the train platform I could scarcely believe my eyes. It seemed as though heaven itself had suddenly smiled down on me."

"Had you not seen me then, when would you have ever showed me your feelings?"

"It would not have been long. I swore I would find a way to speak to you again, no matter what it took. Seeing you on that platform was the embodiment of all I hoped for. I am not a religious man, but if ever I could believe Providence had answered my prayer to see you again, it was on that day."

"And then you kissed me," Margaret said, blushing at the memory.

"Repeatedly," Thornton agreed, with a roguish smile. "I will not apologize for that, though it was completely against every rule of decorum. It seemed there was no other way to convey my feelings at that moment."

"I did not mind," Margaret assured him with a shy smile.

"Hat or no hat, you are adorable with that smile on your face! No, do not blush and turn away. I will remember the proprieties for now, though you do make it hard work."

They continued walking and talking in that way for quite a time, utterly oblivious to anyone or anything around them; until Thornton remembered the letter his mother had given him for Margaret and handed it to her, with an apology for his forgetfulness. Margaret took it with the greatest of pleasure. "This will be my cousin Edith's congratulations on our engagement. I am hoping that she is writing with the date that she, her husband, and my aunt will arrive for the ceremony. Do you mind if I open it now?"

"Not at all; go ahead."

Margaret opened the envelope and began to read with a look of happy anticipation, but as she proceeded further, still walking slowly with Thornton, her look became more and more troubled. At length, reaching the end, she exclaimed, "Oh, what a turn! Such a disappointment! I did not look for this response at all. John, I think perhaps you ought to read this."

Thornton did not wait to be asked twice. Taking it from her hand, he began reading through the flowery, feminine script, written as if in a tremendous hurry.

My darling Margaret,

You are engaged, and it is not to Henry? I have such a headache, and have been nearly sick to my stomach, to learn that you have given yourself to another. My mother, too, is grieved and disappointed.

I am sure it will seem strange to you that I did not return your correspondence earlier, but Sholto has been ill all this week and the captain has been in Liverpool these ten days. With these two circumstances, and even with my mother's help, I was not at leisure to do anything more than comfort and console my son, for he coughed and felt miserably ill all week. I only just opened your letter this morning! Besides this, Henry told us only that you had elected to stay in Milton a while longer with friends; we had no reason to suppose anything amiss or, even with a sick child, you would have heard from me days ago.

Margaret, I cannot help but feel that you are making a terrible mistake by agreeing to marry this Mr. Thornton. Have you not always hated the north and everything in it? Such a dirty, smelly town! Have you not enjoyed London and living in our house, with people who love you? And there must be so many sad memories for you in that terrible place! I feel that I must have failed you miserably in some way or else you would not be so eager to leave us. And London has ever so many plays and concerts and museums which you will never be able to see in a small manufacturing town.

I am very sure that it is still possible for you to marry Henry. If you leave Milton at once, as soon as you receive this letter, and come straight to us in London, I will tell Henry that you realized you made a terrible mistake, and I know he will be so overcome with joy that he will make you an offer straightaway. And Margaret, you must admit that a rising attorney in London is a much more attractive marriage partner than a failed business owner in a small northern town of no importance to anyone at all.

Anyway I will not rest until I hear from you myself, <u>in person</u>, that this is your earnest desire. The captain leaves Liverpool Tuesday next, and I have written to him to ask him to visit you in Milton on his way back to London. He will collect you and bring you home where you belong. My mother says that she will simply not believe you are to marry this Thornton man, as she labels him, until you can talk to her face to face. Come home with the captain, and let us talk all this over sensibly. You may expect to see the captain late Tuesday afternoon.

Your affectionate and remarkably weary cousin,

Edith

Thornton handed the letter back to Margaret with his mouth set in a straight line. "So your family does not approve of me it seems. I am not terribly surprised. I am not a gentleman in the way they expect."

"But you are to be my husband! I would expect them to respect my choice and be more welcoming of anyone I set my heart on. I am not a child who does not know my own mind."

"No doubt they believe I am after your money." This time Margaret heard the tinge of bitterness in his tone, and she pressed his arm consolingly, looking up at his face earnestly.

"I will teach them otherwise; they simply have not come to know you yet. Once they meet you they will love you as I do."

"Not Henry, I do not believe."

Margaret could not help smiling. "No, not Henry; that is not possible; but then he has his own goals in mind."

Thornton looked down at Margaret with grave concern. "Would you wish to delay our wedding, in order to have time to gain your family's support?"

"No!" This exclamation from Margaret was so emphatic that Thornton took comfort in it. He had been afraid that their wedding might be delayed weeks or even months while Margaret tried to convince her family of the certainty of her decision, but it seemed his fear on that subject was groundless.

"I do not wish to delay our wedding on any account; but I must admit that I do not look forward to facing my cousin the captain's objections and arguments, either. He is not a forceful man but he can be remarkably persistent, and I foresee that there will be a great deal of trouble when he comes."

"What can he do against you? You are of age, are you not? He could not prevent your marrying, could he?"

"I am one and twenty, barely. I can marry as I wish, without reference to anybody; but my aunt and cousin are the only family I have besides my brother. I would like to wed without my marriage causing dissension, but I am afraid that convincing them of the strength of my attachment to you may take some time."

"There is an easy solution, my love," Thornton said quietly, folding both of his gloved hands around one of hers, and inclining his head to look directly in her face. "Let us wait no longer to marry, at least no longer than Monday."

"Monday! That is two days from now!" Margaret could scarcely believe her ears. "You are not in earnest."

"Why not? If we marry on Monday we can take the afternoon train to Bath, so that we will be long gone before your cousin arrives. He can hardly argue with an action already taken, particularly when there is no one with whom to argue."

"You cannot be in earnest!"

"I assure you that I am."

"But my cousin! My aunt! They would be so disappointed if I were to take such a serious step without them. I cannot seriously consider it."'

"Would you rather wait to marry until you have convinced them of the strength of our attachment?"

"No." Margaret shook her head emphatically. "I do not wish to wait upon their change in opinion."

"Then will you not consider making this small change in our plans, dearest?" Thornton asked with his most imploring tone. "I know how much you love your family and what their approval means to you. If your cousin arrives before our wedding and tries to persuade you to wait, will you be able to proceed as planned, with no guilt or feeling of regret? I think not. You have a tender heart, the tenderest heart I have ever seen. I do not see how you could escape such a scene without feeling deeply grieved, and to what end? If you still wish to marry me, and if all preparations are well enough in hand, why not carry out your purpose directly?"

"But I would like to have them meet you and come to approve of you before our wedding. Once they know you, I know they will love you as I do. Why do you look at me that way?"

"I am simply delighted to hear you declare your love for me so strongly. I hope you feel compelled to do so very often."

"Vanity! But I will tell you as often as you wish."

"That will be very often, indeed," Thornton assured her; and resisting no longer, he bent down to kiss her lips just once. When he pulled back, the softened, open expression on her face told him that now was the time to press his point. He spoke earnestly.

"Marry me Monday, Margaret. By noon we will be husband and wife. We will travel in the train and be in Bath on Tuesday, and our plans will go forward just as we had already decided from then on. We can spend a few days in Bath and then go to London, and there we will take as much time as you want for me to become acquainted with your family. It may," he finished mischievously, "take a very long time to change their opinions. Consider how long it took you to overcome your prejudice towards the north."

Margaret, although almost overwhelmed by the emotions of the moment, nevertheless remained clear-headed enough to realize that now was the chance to gain her own advantage. She stopped walking as she faced Thornton, meeting his gaze evenly. "I will agree to marry you on Monday on one condition, John."

 "Name it, my love."

"Take my money to open Marlborough Mills again as soon as our wedding trip is over. I will not allow you to have any objections this time. It is my money to do with as I wish, and I wish to invest it in your business. You will not be able to convince me otherwise."

Thornton's eyes narrowed as he looked down at her, measuring her air of determination. "As I said before, you bargain well. I will do as you ask." At her sudden look of delight he added, "*If* you will allow me to repay the loan as soon as possible and then to settle it all on you in a way that will provide for you after my death."

"Then I will be happy to marry you in two days," Margaret answered, her heart pounding hard. As the enormity of her decision washed over her, she let her head rest on Thornton's chest and felt his arms go around her.

"I am about to flout propriety once again," John whispered in her ear as he tilted her face up towards him, "my own dearest Margaret!"

Chapter Ten

A Business Proposition

The preparations which their decision now spurred, the hasty notifications to family and friends, the rapid completion of Margaret's wedding dress, the sudden purchases of food for the wedding breakfast, the reconsideration of the menu, the rush to order flowers--all this can only be imagined by the reader. It is enough to say that Hannah, Margaret, Thornton, and everybody in the house were now fixed with one mind on the goal of the wedding taking place on Monday morning, and that goal kept them thoroughly preoccupied every waking moment.

Thornton experienced some moments of guilt when he realized how much sudden work was now being dropped on the heads of his mother and his intended. He himself had very little to do besides speaking to the parson at his earliest opportunity and securing that man's cooperation. But Hannah and Margaret both assured him that it was no great trouble, and Hannah was remarkably even tempered despite the sudden change in plans. Hearing that Marlborough Mills would soon be operating again probably had something to do with it.

As for Margaret, she proceeded through the rest of Saturday and all of Sunday in a sort of overwhelmed bliss. She did not forget to miss her family, especially Edith, but she was determined not to dwell on anything that might cause unhappiness, and put all of her energy into readying herself to start her new life.

Their preparations were still in rapid progress when Higgins called at the Thornton's house on Sunday afternoon. Thornton welcomed him warmly, advising him to avoid stepping on any square inch of rug if he could, as it might bring down the wrath of the household staff on his unsuspecting head. "And I will ask you to sit with me at the kitchen table, and not in the parlor," he added. "I trust you will understand that conversation in the parlor is impossible today with the windows being cleaned and the pillows being beaten, if you can even find a seat which is not being dusted off at the moment. I suppose you heard that Miss Margaret and I are to marry tomorrow?"

"Aye, and a good thing it is, too," said Higgins, with a broad smile. "I'm thinking it's something as should have taken place a long time ago. A right good match it is."

"I thank you. I hope you'll plan to join us for the ceremony. Margaret would be pleased to have you there."

"In all my best clothes? I'll come as long as you don't think I'll be over-dressed," Higgins replied, grinning down at the humble outfit which served as his best, second best, and everyday suit. "But that is the very reason I came. I'm not sure if I'll see you tomorrow before you leave on your wedding trip, and Mary and I will be leaving as well. We'll not be here when you get back. So I came today to say goodbye, and to thank you for all that the two of you have ever done for us."

"You're leaving Milton? Where are you going?" asked Thornton, his light-hearted mood suddenly turning serious.

"It's like this: there isn't no work for a man like me in a town like this, not with your mill not operating, and I've Boucher's six children to support. I've tried to make a go of it for a bit, but I've got to go to where the work is. It's that plain and simple. I'd have been gone already if Miss Margaret hadn't put in a word for me with you, all that time ago."

"No, you mustn't leave, Higgins." Thornton's mood was instantly restored. "The mill is going to operate again. As soon as we return from our wedding trip, I'll be calling up workers to start the machinery once more. My landlord has insisted that the mills be restored to full profitability right away." He said this last with a mischievous smile for his intended, who had just entered the kitchen in search of the cook and now stood listening intently. She smiled back at him warmly. "So you see there'll be a place for you after all."

"I am glad to hear it. Thank you, master," Higgins said gratefully, and the two shook hands warmly. "That'll be good news for this town, for sure!" he continued. "'Tis an ugly mood out there today, what with the news about Watson and his speculation. I can't understand how a man could make so much money, more than I'll ever see in my lifetime, surely, and turn around and lose it all again. It must be precious hard work to keep money once you have it."

Thornton smiled wryly. "Indeed. Many a man who makes it quickly finds that it leaves in much the same manner."

"Now," Higgins said earnestly, "if I ever had half the fortune some of these masters have, I'd be a bit more careful with what I did with it, that's for sure. I'd be putting my capital to work in a proper way, by building up my business for the future, and setting a good amount aside for the hard times. No matter how careful a man may be, hard times always come sooner or later. I'd put my mind to building up against them, not trying to extend myself more."

"You'd be a proper master, Higgins, of that I have no doubt," Thornton said, frowning as a new idea entered his mind.

"I can't never be a master, though; ain't never been a master in the union yet," Higgins answered with a knowing smile. "Anyway, that's not for me. I'm not book learned the way you are, nor do I know the ways of ledgers and contracts and such. I reckon I'm happy enough being a worker, as my father was before me."

"What do you mean by there being an ugly mood today?" Margaret asked, reverting back to Higgins' words when she first entered the room. "Do you mean in the town?"

Higgins shook his head, troubled. "There's already a powerful lot of people out of work in Milton. Some people have been out long enough to be getting desperate if something doesn't change. It's like the strike all over again, almost, except that the workers then at least had their strike wage, little though it was. Now they have nothing. Watson's speculation failing wouldn't be the news they want to hear."

"Do you mean there would be a riot?"

"'Twouldn't surprise me. I understand half the masters in town was with Watson on his scheme. If he goes down, maybe the others will too."

Thornton shook his head. "I don't think even Watson himself will fail, let alone the other masters. He protected himself by demanding security, and that will probably be his salvation. His principal, I think, has been largely regained; it is only a fraction of the original which is still at risk. Mind you, even that fraction is a large number. But I still think he'll pull through without too much trouble."

"Then mayhap I'll go and give your opinion to the men I know," Higgins suggested, "now that I know I'll not be leaving town after all. I'll be right glad to work at Marlborough Mills again." At Margaret's questioning look, he explained his original purpose in calling, finishing with, "The men here respect your word, sir. If I tell them that Thornton says the other masters are safe, it'll go a long way towards quieting down what's brewing out there. And if I can tell them you'll be opening the mill again it'll do even more."

"You may tell them my opinion, and welcome, if you think it will help. I would rather not announce anything about Marlborough Mills just yet. But in any event you must promise to attend our wedding tomorrow. We would not have it otherwise."

"Yes, Nicholas, please come," Margaret urged him. "I understand that we owe our present good understanding in part to some timely remarks you made to Mr. Thornton. We must have you there, along with Mary."

"Aye, we'll come, and gladly. I'm happy to have been of some small service to the both of you, after all you've done for me and mine, and I'm glad I'll not have to leave Milton after all. And now I think I ought to be on my way, so I can try to make myself look presentable before tomorrow morning."

"I wish you would stay a moment instead, Higgins," said Thornton, coming to a sudden decision. "I have a business proposition for you."

∞

"A model employee indeed," Margaret commented to Thornton an hour later, half-laughing, after Higgins, grateful and disbelieving, had shaken Thornton's hand one more time and finally made his exit. "The other masters will say that you are rewarding Higgins for his impertinent ways."

"The other masters will think as they wish, but they won't find the quality of workers I mean to have. I wish Higgins would have agreed to be foreman. My man Lentz has already taken work elsewhere, and I'll be hard put to fill those shoes. But Higgins will never leave the union, and I can only respect his loyalty to his brothers."

"Is there really such a position as floor supervisor?" Margaret asked doubtfully. "Or did you create the position for Higgins, just to please me?"

"I didn't think you would have any objection, my love."

"Of course not."

"But it was not just to please you. Higgins is no common weaver. He is a remarkably clever man who brings his brains with him to work every day; his talents are wasted in a lower position. I will rely on him to manage the floor, to stop trouble before it starts, to let me know if he thinks there's a more efficient way to carry out our operations. He'll give me his honest opinion, which is more than I can say of many men. And if there is trouble brewing with the union, I hope he'll feel free to tell me of it before it becomes an issue. So you see, it is a sound business decision."

"It is a kind act, carried out by a man who cares for his workers,"

Margaret corrected him, not accepting his modest diversion. "The extra pay will help him considerably in caring for Boucher's children."

"They deserve the care. It's not their fault what their father did, and it is good of Higgins to take them on. The first thing I'll ask Higgins to do is to find Mason and make him an offer, and that way little James will not be needing to show up at our door for food every morning."

"You have grown soft towards your employees," Margaret observed with a proud smile.

Thornton answered warmly, "If I have, it is your fault," and followed his words with several convincing tokens of his affection.

Chapter Eleven

"You Would Have Been The One"

The wedding day, anxiously awaited yet arriving suddenly, dawned with a fine sun, a light breeze, and no clouds on the horizon until about eight, when a growing stormy mass in the east promised a heavy downpour later. Outside Margaret's window a single lark sang while she finished dressing, its clear song a happy omen, she thought, for the day to come.

By nine in the morning two carriages decorated with flowers and streamers stood in front of the Thornton residence, ready to convey Thornton to the church first and then Margaret and Hannah some minutes later. Thornton was supervising the loading of his and Margaret's carpetbags onto the top of the first carriage. Since the date of the wedding had been so accelerated Margaret had not secured a hotel room after all, but she still desired to arrive at the church separately from Thornton so that they could then leave as one. After the ceremony the new couple would proceed directly from the church to the Outwood station in order to start on their wedding trip immediately, but their guests would return to Thornton House for a wedding breakfast. Hannah, inside, was giving brisk instructions to the cook and two maids, who could hardly wait for the wedding party to leave so that they might have a few minute's peace before the expected guests arrived.

Margaret had already finished all possible preparations. She was sitting restlessly in the parlor, listening to the sounds in the house, anxious and pensive; the hands on the clock had never seemed to move so slowly. As Margaret watched the clock hands, marking every minute with the silent sentinels, her mind traveled back to the first time she had ever seen the man she was about to marry.

He had been on the factory work floor, his dark suit and hair a sharp contrast to the white fluff in the air and on every possible surface. It was impossible not to remember the anger and righteous indignation she had first felt towards him, her own air of moral superiority, and the naïve certainty of her own innocent convictions. She recoiled in shame to remember how she had shrunk back when he offered his hand in amity, how she had steadfastly avoided any advance towards friendship on his part. She had been so resolute, so determined in her efforts to quit herself of anything and everything connected with the man she believed to be the cold, harsh master of Marlborough Mills, John Thornton.

But then she had slowly, oh so slowly, against her will, developed a reluctant respect for him. Who would not do so, after hearing of the way he had been forced to take on leadership of his family and provide for them from a young age? Who would not admire the compulsion which had driven him relentlessly from poverty to riches by dint of nothing more than his own hard work and self-denial? Who could deny his strength of character, the honorable reputation gained among his own peers?

When had admiration changed to sympathy, and sympathy to warm affection? She could not say; she only knew that the change had been gradual, a result of seeing his kindness and concern reflected to her and her family daily. She had slowly come to regret every deficit of civility she had carried out, and become desirous of his good opinion only after it had seemed too late to ever gain. And now, here she was, his chosen and beloved, and soon to be his wife!

Their relationship, already so changeable and so unlikely in its outcome, would alter forever today, this time into one of the closest possible intimacy. She hoped to make him happy; she prayed quietly to be worthy of his admiration and devotion. She would strive to imitate, though she felt she could never duplicate, his assiduous care for those he loved.

Just then she heard Thornton's quick footstep in the hallway. Unable to stop herself she glanced up, expecting to see him walk quickly by the room; instead he broke all convention by peering into the room for her, his eyes seeking her out hesitantly. His face relaxed at her welcoming expression, and he came to her side instantly to take her hand in his, eyes shining with pleasure. "They say it is bad luck for the groom to see the bride before the wedding, but I could not help myself. I had to see you just once. How lovely you are!"

"It is beautiful, this dress," Margaret answered with some embarrassment, smoothing down the front of it with her free hand, her fingers lingering on the soft fabric.

"I would say more the wearer," Thornton answered, his eyes not leaving her face as he continued to gaze at her. "Are you ready for this step, my love? I confess I wish the ceremony already over. I could hardly sleep last night for thinking of it."

"I had trouble sleeping as well."

"You are trembling!" Thornton said in surprise, feeling the tension in Margaret's body being relayed down to her very fingertips, although it did not show on her face. Margaret could not answer, gazing down at the floor while she clutched John's hand ever more tightly. Thornton continued to quietly observe her.

"Your emotions must be very strong this morning," he finally said. "I cannot imagine what you must be feeling right now, preparing to leave your life as an unattached woman and join yourself to a wholly new family, without the support of your own family by your side. It must be overwhelming, even to one as strong as you are."

"I do not feel strong, John," she answered quietly, still looking down. "You must not call me that. I have courage enough for myself, sometimes, but not for others. I fear I am wholly inadequate to be called your partner in life."

"So says the woman who threw herself in front of a crowd of angry rioters to save me, before she even cared for me!" Thornton reproved her, affectionately. "It is only this state of marriage which is intimidating you now, but it is the very role in which you are most suited to be my partner. Have faith in my love for you, dearest; all will be well. Besides," he added humorously, "I need you to calm my own nerves. I am not myself at all."

"You!" Margaret finally dared to look up at her groom's face. "You are completely cool and collected; nothing ever shakes you."

"That is not true. I tremble whenever I think of how unlikely it was that you would ever learn to love me, and when I recall how close I came to losing you forever. I fear that I will not be enough to make you happy in the way you deserve."

"You do make me happy, John, and I know you will continue to do so," Margaret answered, eager to reassure him. "I just hope that I can do the same for you."

"Of course you will. Have faith in our love, dearest, and all will be well."

"I will try, John," Margaret answered, feeling a little reassured, and she allowed him to pull her against him, embracing her for the last time before their wedding. It was in this pose that Hannah found them, entering the room to look for her son.

"It is considered bad form to see the bride before the wedding," she commented drily, "but I suppose it is rather late to think of such a thing now. John, it is time for you to go to the church. We will be following you directly."

Thornton released Margaret with the greatest of reluctance. "I will see you in a few minutes, love. Take this--I have been waiting to give it to you for some time." He gave her a small envelope from his pocket, pressing it into her hand while he looked at her one last time. With his mother watching he could not kiss his bride the way he wanted to, not yet, but that would be remedied shortly. With a final encouraging smile he turned on his heel and left the room, and a minute later Hannah and Margaret saw his carriage go past the parlor window, to the cheers and raucous good wishes of a dozen or so passers-by.

Margaret did not wait to open Thornton's gift. With trembling fingers she slipped her fingernail under the edge of the envelope, and as the pages fell apart a small yellow object fell to the floor. Margaret retrieved it to find that it was one of the yellow Helstone roses, a twin to the one he had given her at the railroad station, its petals carefully dried to perfection. She lifted the flower to her face and inhaled deeply. Somehow, Thornton's simple gesture combined with the sweet fragrance reassured her more than any words ever could, and she felt her hands cease their nervous trembling. Joyfully, she tucked the small flower in amongst the larger white blossoms in her wedding bouquet and smiled broadly at Hannah. "I am ready now."

Never one to overlook details, Hannah called her maid into the room for a final check of Margaret's hair and gown before moving to cover her face with the veil. But instead of letting the maid complete her task, Hannah took the veil in her own hands, looking at Margaret with solemn dignity before speaking.

"I want you to know something, Margaret," she said in a voice heavy with emotion. "I know that I could not have picked John's wife for him. It is not the custom among people of our class, and John is far too independent to allow such an arrangement even if it were. But if I could have picked the woman who would share his life," she paused, looking Margaret directly in the eye, "you would have been the one. There can be no one more perfect for him. Love him and care for him as only you can, and you will be very happy together." She embraced Margaret and kissed her solemnly before lowering the veil, and Margaret felt as if a ceremony nearly as momentous as the wedding itself had just taken place.

Margaret and Hannah now moved outdoors and took their places in their own carriage, encouraged and cheered on by the same small crowd that had applauded Thornton and now lingered to see them off. But in this case, Margaret's shy beauty and air of reserve created a more respectful response. A general murmur of approval followed her into the carriage as the door was closed, and from the window she could see many faces smiling upon her as if in blessing. The ride to the church was not long, and almost before she knew where she was, Margaret was climbing out of the carriage to stand in front of the outer doors to the church, which were thrown wide open at their arrival. Overhead, she heard the church bells begin to peal out.

"It is time," said Hannah, adjusting Margaret's veil one last time. "I will go in and sit down, and you will follow whenever you wish."

Margaret could imagine Thornton's anxiousness, standing by himself at the front of the sanctuary. "I will come as soon as you are seated."

"It looks as though the rain will hold off until after the ceremony," Hannah commented, looking up at the sky. She seemed strangely reluctant to leave Margaret's side. "Are you sure you do not want one of the masters to walk you down the aisle? I'm sure any of them would be honored to be asked."

"No. I am coming as myself." Margaret's voice was gentle but firm. If her father or Mr. Bell could not be there, she would give herself away.

"As you wish. Bless you, my child." Hannah's voice had grown tender, and she looked at Margaret one last time with eyes that were shining suspiciously. With a final look she passed through the inner church doors and disappeared into the darkness inside. One of the door attendants, watching after her, turned and nodded significantly to Margaret. It was time.

Margaret passed through the inner doors and stood for a moment at the head of the aisle, allowing her eyes to adjust to the comparative darkness inside before proceeding further. At first, she could make out nothing beyond the light from a dozen candles arranged behind the altar, beautiful in their radiant simplicity. Then she could make out vague shadows of the handful of people who had come to watch the ceremony.

Gradually, more details began to stand out--Nicholas and Mary on the bride's side, turned towards with her expectant, joyous faces; a dozen or so masters and their wives on the groom's side, looking at her with kindly expressions; Watson and Fanny sitting in the row in front of Hannah, faces rigidly forward while Watson wiped copious sweat from his brow and Fanny vigorously fanned herself; Hannah, looking up with pride and an open smile; *and John*, his hands nervously clenched tight, seeming as though he were on the verge of running down the aisle and to her side.

From the moment Margaret saw Thornton, all else faded from view. His smile was all that mattered; she was lost, swallowed up completely within his gaze. She proceeded carefully yet steadily up the aisle, moving directly to him and not hesitating to place her hand in his. He clasped it tightly and turned with her to face the parson together.

And so they were married.

Chapter Twelve

"Ruined!"

It was done. The moment he had desired for so long had arrived and now washed over him, leaving behind a glow of incredulous joy. Margaret was his. From now on, it would be the two of them facing the world together, he and Margaret, not just the solitary John Thornton.

"Ladies and gentlemen, may I present Mr. and Mrs. John Thornton," the parson intoned formally, and the newly married couple stood close together, facing their audience as a married couple for the first time. To general sounds of approval and wide smiles all around, they walked up the aisle and back to the nave, where they stood together to greet their guests. The outer doors were still open and to their surprise, a light rain had begun to fall outside.

"My darling Margaret, I did not even realize we had clouds in the sky today," Thornton told her tenderly. "I have been thinking too much of you to notice anything else. A monsoon might have struck and I would have paid it no mind."

"Your mother and I saw the rain coming, but she did not think it would start so soon."

Thornton shook his head. "It is no matter. Nothing can dampen my spirits today." And he kissed her fervently, their first kiss as husband and wife, simply because he could.

"John, really," his mother said severely, joining them as she finished her own walk back up the aisle. "Such displays of affection are out of place in church. Wait until you can be alone with your bride!" But she looked more amused than angry and her words were missing their usual barb. She embraced both Thornton and Margaret warmly as Watson and Fanny approached.

"Congratulations, Miss Hale," Fanny said petulantly, offering Margaret a cold kiss on the cheek. "Or I suppose you'll allow me to call you Margaret now, since we are sisters? I'm sure that I hope you and John will be happy together."

"We plan to be so," Margaret replied gently, wishing to be on friendlier terms with her new sister. "I would be honored if you would call me Margaret."

"And you may call me Fanny," the other woman replied without warmth. "You're going off to Bath for your wedding trip, aren't you? Enjoy London when you go through it; it's not likely you'll be back any time soon. Once you and John are properly settled in at the house, I imagine I'll be over to call on you."

"I will look forward to it," Margaret said, looking next at Fanny's husband as he approached. "Mr. Watson, we are so pleased to have you at our wedding." Next to her, Thornton tensed.

"It was well done. Many happy wishes, I'm sure." Watson's voice was distant, his expression distracted, and he once again held his handkerchief to his brow, wiping away great drops of perspiration. He moved on abruptly to Thornton with no further words for Margaret, leaving her nonplussed. Had she offended the man in some way? But he did not seem offended as he shook Thornton's hand politely, merely in a state of considerable anxiety, his face red and puffy, his uneasy eyes refusing to meet Thornton's for any length of time. He looked as if he would rather be anywhere else at that moment. Perhaps he was ashamed of what had passed between him and his brother-in-law just a few days previously. Margaret frowned as she looked after him, but she had no chance to speak with him further as another well-wisher came to her side. Thornton's eyes darkened and his lips tightened as he accepted Watson's hand, but if he noticed anything amiss he kept his observations to himself.

There was no opportunity for private conversation just now anyway. They were all coming, the remaining masters, the parson's wife, a handful of other friends, and Nicholas with Mary, all full of good wishes and assuring the new couple of their hopes for every future happiness. The small group filled up the nave entirely, but no one moved out into the church yard. The rain was coming down more steadily now, and by unspoken consent, the guests were waiting for Thornton and Margaret to finish greeting everyone and to depart for the train station before they would call for their own carriages and proceed to the Thornton's house. Already Thornton's carriage was slowly making its way through the church yard gates and towards the door, its wheels leaving deep tracks in the dampening ground.

"Our bags--are they already at the station?" Margaret asked her husband when she saw the carriage, noting the absence of the items Thornton had seen placed there earlier.

"Yes, I had the driver take them to Outwood already, to wait for us. And it's a good thing, too, considering this sudden rain. I would not like our things to be ruined for being wet. Margaret, my love, are you ready to leave? Have you had a chance to greet everyone?"

"Yes, I am ready if you are. I just—" but whatever Margaret was going to say next was forever lost. Little James Mason, his jacket and hat already beginning to drip, had just darted into the church yard with his arms full of the daily paper. She could not help smiling at the bedraggled child.

"James, do come in out of the rain for a moment," she urged him, motioning him forward.

"No, thank you," he said, smiling widely, "I'd make a horrid mess all over the carpet. I just came to give Mr. Thornton his paper. Mr. Thornton!" he called. "You'll be wanting your paper, sir!"

"The paper!" scoffed Hannah as Thornton stepped towards the lad. "Can't you see you've interrupted a wedding, child? Mr. Thornton has more important matters on his mind. We'll be wanting no paper today."

"No, mother, it is all right," Thornton said with an affectionate smile for his bride. Today nothing could raise his ill-will. "Give me a paper, James, and take this payment for it as a gift on our wedding day." He handed the child a much larger coin than would be expected, and James looked at him with a broad grin.

"Thank you, sir! And congratulations!" He touched his hat and began to move off again. But before he could even leave the church yard, Watson had spied the paper in Thornton's hand and lunged for it.

"Thornton, I must see it! Let me see it!" Too quick for protest, he seized the newspaper and grasped it with trembling hands, his eyes sweeping over the headlines. He tore open the first page and looked inside, scanning the text rapidly while Thornton, Margaret and Hannah looked on, astonished by his precipitous manner. Watson quickly turned page after page until his eyes, glancing down the left hand side of the page, stopped suddenly half way down. His widening eyes moved over the same lines several times; he gasped, closed his eyes, uttered an oath, and opened his eyes again to repeat the exercise, as though he could not believe what he had read the first time. Then he slowly folded the pages together with great care and handed them back to Thornton with as much dignity as he could muster. He muttered something incomprehensible; Margaret thought she saw a shudder pass through him as the unknown words passed his lips.

Fanny must have understood what her husband said; she paled and grasped his arm. "You must sit down, Watson, you must sit down. Come and sit here. You are very ill. Mother!" she suddenly cried. "Watson is ill!"

It was true; Watson was clutching at his heart and beginning to crumple. In a flash of movement Thornton and Nicholas each took one of his arms and eased his considerable form onto a nearby settee, where Watson collapsed awkwardly, gasping for breath. Fanny tearfully stood next to him. "Somebody go for a doctor!'

"I'll go!" cried James, who stood nearby, watching with wide eyes, papers still clutched to his chest. Watson's sudden exclamation and abrupt behavior had caught his attention, and he stood just outside the foyer, looking on in horrified fascination. "I know just where he is!"

"Yes, go!" Margaret urged him, suddenly stirred to action. "Go, and do not return without him! Have you a cordial?" she asked Hannah as James sped away in the rain, his feet flinging mud behind him.

Hannah was already removing a small bottle from the reticule which accompanied her everywhere. "Here, Watson, drink this. And Fanny, you should use it too," she added, seeing the look on her daughter's face. "Is it not enough to have one person ill? You need not make yourself sick as well." Fanny sank down onto the seat next to her husband, looking scarcely less ill than he. Beside her, Watson was trying with trembling fingers to remove the stopper from the restorative; his color had returned somewhat, but he still gasped for breath. Hannah pulled the stopper out impatiently and Watson drank immediately.

"Can anyone get a burnt feather?" Margaret asked, her clear voice carrying strongly throughout the nave. In response the parson, pushing his way through the small group, produced a feather which he thrust briefly into a nearby candle; Fanny held the feather to her nose while the others watched with deep concern.

Thornton, unneeded for the moment, had sought out the page his brother in law had been reading. When he looked up at Margaret and Hannah again his face was grim.

"Simon Diego's government has fallen," he said quietly. "He has fled the country, and his followers with him. The revolution is lost."

Watson had recovered his power of speech, and now everyone could hear his words clearly as he gasped, over and over again, "Ruined! We are all ruined!"

Thornton glanced uncertainly between the paper in his hands and his brother-in-law, still distraught, and knelt down next to him. "I do not understand you, Watson," he said, not loudly, but with all eyes on him in the drama of the moment. "You have security; you recovered your principal. In the end you have lost nothing but the gains you might have made. Your present funds are not touched. You cannot be ruined."

Watson shook his head emphatically no. "The cacao beans were rotted, destroyed by a fungus in port. To keep our venture solvent I had to pledge our personal property against another loan. My mills, my house, the very carriage I rode in to get here—it is all gone!"

"Watson, you deuced idiot!" Thornton could not help exclaiming, but a look from Margaret restrained him from saying anything else, and they all stood together as the reality of their sudden misfortune, like the rain outside, poured down heavily upon them.

Chapter Thirteen

Many Changes

A good half hour passed before the doctor arrived on the scene. Hannah knelt on one side of Watson while Thornton kept his post on the other, leaving Margaret to comfort and quiet the distraught Fanny. Watson, worsening by the minute, lay back fully on the settee, his bulk leaving no room for his hysterical wife, his lips turning blue as his breathing became more and more shallow. Despite his distress he insisted on asking Thornton to convey his regrets to the other masters whose fortunes had likewise disappeared. It was only then that Thornton realized, with a thrill of horror, that Watson had taken pledges of personal property from other investors as well. If true, Watson would not be the only man laid low on this day. He wished he could press Watson for more details but he did not dare to do so under the circumstances, and instead urged him to be as quiet as possible.

"He is going to die, isn't he? He is going to die, and I will be left alone, without a penny to my name!" were Fanny's words, which Margaret did her best to contain by pressing Fanny's head to her shoulder, comforting her the way a mother would a child. Watson gave no sign of recognizing his wife's distress. At last his voice ceased and he closed his eyes. Thornton quickly laid a hand on his chest and leaned down to detect sounds of breathing.

"He is unconscious," Thornton assured his horrified mother, "not dead. It is better this way. He should not be exerting himself by so much speaking."

"He needs to be moved," Hannah answered, looking dismayed, as well she might given the rapid change of circumstances. "He cannot be helped here."

"We dare not move him until the doctor arrives--ah, Donaldson," Thornton added, for the doctor's carriage was just coming around the corner, approaching the church at a rapid pace. Donaldson leaped out almost before the wheels of the carriage had stopped turning and pushed his way through the small group still assembled. He made a quick examination of the patient for several anxious minutes and then stood up, his face grave with concern.

"I am afraid, sir," he said, looking at Mr. Brown, who had presided over the wedding so shortly before, "that we will have to trespass on your hospitality for Watson's sake. Let a litter be arranged to carry him into the parsonage and I will arrange for a nurse to come to him. He cannot be moved farther than that without danger."

"But will he recover?" cried Fanny, clutching to Margaret's arms with both hands. "Is he going to live, or will I be made a widow so young?"

"God only knows," Donaldson replied somberly, shaking his head. "His heart has been affected, but whether it is from a real weakness in the muscle or from the shock of his business failure, I cannot tell. In the end it may come to the same thing, but I hope not. I will do all I can. We will know much more in a day or two, if he is still with us then."

"You have heard of his business failure?" Hannah asked in a low voice.

"The news is spreading all over town," Donaldson replied grimly, but he did not have time to elaborate. For the next hour or so the arrangements for Watson's care consumed his attention, as well as everyone else's. With considerable trouble Watson was lifted and carried through the rain into the living room of the small, neat parsonage only a few feet away. The remaining wedding guests had made subdued farewells and departed for their homes, their hushed voices already recalling the shocking turn of events amongst themselves; and conjecturing as to the extent of the hurt the town of Milton would suffer, now that all hope from the speculation was gone.

Inside the parsonage Margaret and Fanny sat numbly while Thornton and Hannah, with Donaldson, made arrangements for nursing care and other needs. At length Mr. Brown turned to the two of them.

"Mrs. Watson, a room shall be made available here for your comfort for the duration of your husband's stay, and my wife will be pleased to offer you whatever help she can."

"Is there room here for me as well?" Hannah asked him anxiously. "I need to stay with Fanny."

"If you do not mind sharing quarters with your daughter then there will be room. I am afraid, however, that there is no accommodation here for Mr. and Mrs. Thornton, as my house is not large."

"There is no need for apology, sir," Thornton assured him. "You are more generous already than I could have hoped for. I trust that my mother and sister, and Watson, will not need to intrude upon your hospitality for long. Mother, we will need to send a messenger to the Watson's and to our house to bring your things. Margaret—" and here Thornton looked at his wife for the first time in several minutes. His expression was one of deep regret. "I do not think I can leave my mother and sister here alone at such a time. They will need me close at hand. There will be no wedding trip for us just now."

"Of course not," Margaret said at once, having already reached the same conclusion on her own. "We must give your family all the support we can. You must not even think of leaving them." Thornton thanked her with his eyes, but his mind was too preoccupied to say anything else to her.

"John, it would make the most sense if you and Margaret were to go and get our things from both houses and bring them back here to us. I will stay with Fanny," Hannah said, looking vastly relieved. And so the arrangements were quickly made. Thornton assured his mother that they would return as soon as possible, and then he and Margaret made the hasty trip across town to the Watson's house, all thought of the wedding trip long gone.

What a difference a few hours could make! Had it been only this morning that they had prepared so happily for their wedding and traveled to the church with such joyful anticipation? It felt like a lifetime ago, and although the rain had slowed and the clouds were starting to lift, the day seemed darker than ever before as they drove through the muddy streets, with occasional brief outbursts still falling from above.

Margaret looked out of the carriage at the passing town as they made their way to the spacious home shared by Fanny and her husband. All around her rose homes and businesses in various states of prosperity, all in different shapes and sizes, and used by people in many different classes of life; and yet all of them, in some way, were affected by the mills! A family with no income could ill afford to pay rent, let alone the other small pleasures of life. The chandler hawking his beeswax candles would feel a drop in income no less than the seller of tall silk hats; the bookseller must be as alarmed as the wagon wright. Not a family in the town would be untouched by this disaster. How far did the damage go, and when would they find out its extent?

Some of the buildings they were driving by now were undoubtedly Margaret's own holdings, part of the bequest left to her by Mr. Bell. She had seen the lists of the properties involved but could recall nothing specific at the moment, and she could not help wondering how her own holdings would be affected. But no matter how she was affected, she and John would be much better off than many of the people whose homes they were now passing.

Thornton's eyes were troubled as he looked straight ahead, while the carriage sped on its way, his expression brooding. But he did remember his wife's presence enough to reach for one of her hands and clasp it tightly within his own, and she felt the thrill of the strength and protection he offered her at that moment. No matter what else happened, they were married, and they would not be separated under any circumstances. For now, that was enough.

They stayed only a brief time at the Watson's home, a wide town house with detailed bric-a-brac, Fanny's especial love, on ostentatious display in every room. A suit of armor stood gaudily in the foyer, polished to a high shine, and costly hothouse flowers filled a table in every room that Margaret could see. None of it did any good now, as clothing and personal items for Fanny's immediate use were quickly assembled by a maid, packed in a carpetbag, and handed to Margaret, who left with Thornton as rapidly as they had arrived.

The next stop was John's home, as Margaret called it in her mind, but then she remembered with a jolt that it was now her home as well. She would not live with her aunt or her cousin in town ever again. These walls here in Milton would see the next stage of her life play out and would be witness to the fulfillment of her greatest hopes and wishes, and perhaps disappointments as well. She would have a hand in the ordering of the home, in arranging its menus and entertainments, and welcoming visitors as the new mistress of the Thornton house. And tonight she would share a bed with her husband for the first time.

Some of this must have crossed Thornton's mind as well, for he took one of her hands in his and raised it to his lips, caressing it gently. His eyes were warm and tender looking down at her as he said, "I wish that your homecoming was under better circumstances, Margaret. Welcome to your new home, Mrs. Thornton."

"Wherever you are is my home," she answered, allowing herself to be lost inside his gaze again.

"Are you sure you will not regret living with me in Milton? When this crisis is past, we might consider moving to town instead if you would like."

"No, John!" she protested at once. "I cannot imagine being with you anywhere else. You are a part of Milton, and it is a part of you. You must live here; the energy and drive of this town is in your very blood. You would be miserable anywhere else."

"I would be miserable only if I were without you," he corrected, "wherever that might be."

"You are a part of Milton and it is a part of you. I could not have one without the other."

Her husband's smile widened into something more brilliant than she had ever seen on his face before. "In that case, let me repeat--welcome home, Margaret Thornton." He kissed her with more tenderness than she had ever received from him previously while they stood on the steps together for a moment, and then he led her inside.

Chapter Fourteen

No Waiting

A lesser woman might have resented the circumstances in which Margaret now found herself, returning from her wedding without the benefit of a wedding trip, having to take on the responsibilities of the house without the aid, advice and guidance of her mother-in-law; and besides this, having to assist her new husband in an unfolding crisis of the first magnitude. And indeed, Margaret did feel the disappointment of the loss of some of her plans. But she was too practical to dwell on what could not be changed, and if she did sigh once or twice, it was only as she worked steadily and without complaint to help her new family.

Margaret's first duty after changing out of her wedding dress was to oversee the disposal of the fine breakfast that would not be enjoyed by their wedding guests after all. So much food, and all of it so appealing! It would not do to waste a single bite of any of it. She directed that a good portion of it first be bundled up to deliver to the parsonage, enough for Hannah, Fanny, the Brown family, and the immediate needs of Donaldson and the nurse he would provide. If they must invade Mr. Brown's home, she decided, at least they could make their invasion a little more welcome by such a gesture. The remainder of the food would stay at the Thornton's house to be consumed by the servants at their leisure. After that she also began to consider what items Hannah would need for her stay at the parsonage.

Thornton, too, was preoccupied. He sent one of the servants to the railroad station to retrieve the baggage which was to have gone on ahead of them to Bath--it would never do to have the items make their way there now, unaccompanied. He also sat down to begin to write out a plan of action with regards to Watson's business, and he sent word to the foreman of Watson's mill, a man he knew slightly, asking him to call on Thornton at his earliest possible convenience. Arrangements would have to be made to determine, as quickly as possible, how viable Hayleigh Mills still was. As far as Thornton knew Watson had no male heirs, leaving Thornton as the most likely overseer of his affairs for the immediate future.

Though they did not know this, while Margaret and Thornton arranged matters inside the house, word was spreading on the streets about the probable failure of many of the mill masters. Not that the exact number of affected masters was certain--it was all conjecture, based on who had been seen with whom in public, or was known to have invested with Watson in the past. The projected number grew as the day went on, and as the number grew so did the degree of confidence with which each man's opinion was stated as fact. In the late morning it was rumored that half a dozen or so mills might have to be shuttered in the next month or so. By mid-afternoon a good number of shopkeepers, who had heard of the matter from people who entered their shops, were convinced that at least a dozen would feel the impact within a fortnight. And by late afternoon, when the mill workers themselves were just leaving their shifts, the number had grown to at least a dozen manufacturers who would certainly not last out the week--perhaps as many as a score.

It was just before dusk when Thornton and Margaret, laden with food, clothing and other sundries, made the short, dismal trip back to the parsonage. Donaldson had tended to his patient for some time but left shortly before their arrival, replaced by his trained nurse. Thornton and Margaret stayed with Hannah and Fanny only a brief time, long enough to see that Watson's condition had not changed but not long enough to impose on the crowded conditions in the home. A makeshift curtain had been hung to separate Watson's bed from the rest of the living room, leaving little room for anyone to sit.

"Will you be all right, mother?" Thornton asked Hannah, reluctant to leave her alone in such circumstances. "Would you like me to send one of the servants to stay with you tonight?"

"There would be no room," Hannah said wearily, glancing around at her surroundings. Fatigue was already beginning to take its toll on her. "Fanny and I will sit with Watson in turns tonight. The nurse will sit in the chair next to his bed, while Fanny and I will take our turn on the bed in the spare bedroom just there." She indicated a room immediately adjacent. "We are all cared for--you need not worry. And this is still your wedding day after all. Do not give us a second thought. Go home with your bride and we will see you tomorrow."

Thornton had to be satisfied with these arrangements, since nothing else was possible. "Send word at once if you need anything at all. We will return as soon as we can." He and Margaret embraced Hannah and assured the stupefied Fanny of their support and then made their way home, leaving the two women to their lonely vigil.

Back at the Thornton house, a message was waiting for Thornton from the foreman of Hayleigh Mills, and he went into the parlor at once to read it and compose a response. In his absence Margaret made her way upstairs and laid her hand on the door of the bedroom that was now hers, wondering what she would find inside when she opened the door. The servants had been occupied all day long due to the sudden change of plans, and she could not imagine when or if they would have found the time to make up Margaret's bed for her, considering the fact that they had not expected either her or Thornton to be at home this evening. For that matter, Thornton's bed might also still need to be arranged. Resolutely she turned the handle of her bedroom door and went inside.

She saw at once that the servants had outdone themselves. Her bed--the bed which she and John would presumably share this night--was made up with a white counterpane and matching pillows, the covers turned back invitingly. Someone had thought to display her wedding bouquet on the dresser, and several bouquets of matching flowers were in vases arranged throughout the room, lending their sweet fragrance to the air. Her dressing gown and nightgown were carefully arranged at the foot of the bed, ready for her use, and the whole atmosphere of the room was one of homey tranquility. Best of all, the single yellow Helstone rose which had been tucked inside her bouquet lay serenely on one pillow, beckoning to her with its familiarity.

There was no need to bathe before bed, as she had already bathed early in the morning. With care and a certain amount of trepidation, she changed swiftly out of her clothes and into her night ensemble, pausing to carefully hang her dress in the wardrobe. Then she let her hair down and brushed it out loosely in front of the mirror, gratified to find that all her personal belongings had been unpacked and arranged neatly in her dresser drawers. No detail, it seemed, had been overlooked in the servant's efforts to welcome their new mistress. Now she had only to wait.

Would Thornton come to her tonight? How much had he influenced the careful arrangements in her room, the romantic details all around her, and how much had been the servants' own initiative? Despite the welcoming air of the room, he might be too careworn and worried, or he might think her too distracted, to carry out their union tonight. He might believe that he would impose on her by seeking out her presence. Perhaps that was why he was still below stairs and she was alone here. But then a light knock sounded on the door. She rose swiftly and went to it, taking a deep breath as she turned the knob.

Margaret had no idea of the beautiful image she presented as she stood in the doorway of her bedroom, the soft light of the lamp just behind her glowing softly on her skin. Everything about her seemed to be illuminated--her rosy cheeks, the soft smoothness of her neck, the light shining in waves on her dark hair, the delicate shine in her eyes. Never since the night of the Thornton's annual dinner party had she looked so desirable, and he felt himself drawn towards her as never before. But he hesitated.

"May I come in?" he asked formally, barely able to speak in front of this lovely vision.

"Please, do," Margaret answered, hiding her disappointment at her husband's restrained manner. She stepped aside to allow him room to enter, and then closed the door behind him.

Thornton's eyes immediately went to the bed behind her, but he glanced around the rest of the room briefly before asking Margaret, "Your room--is it satisfactory? Is everything as you would like it to be?"

"It is lovely," Margaret assured him with a shy smile, "as lovely as if I had arranged it myself. It could not be more perfect."

"I am glad it pleases you," Thornton said, still standing a short distance away from her. He made no move to close the gap.

"Even to the flowers, it is perfect. I was delighted to see my yellow Helstone rose waiting for me on the pillow."

He smiled. "I asked the servants to arrange it that way."

She looked down at the floor, feeling more self-conscious than ever before. "It was thoughtful of you. Indeed, the room could not be more perfect, unless there were one improvement made."

Thornton was instantly alert. "What might that be?"

"It needs you," Margaret said boldly, lifting her head to look directly at her husband, ignoring the furious blush rising to her cheeks. "I will not feel truly married until we have shared this room together."

Thornton did move then, closing the space between them with one step. He reached out to caress her cheek lightly with one hand, just as he had that day on the train platform. "Are you sure? It has been a long day. I would not blame you if you wish to delay the start of this part of our relationship." Despite his words, his thumb continued caressing her cheek, and he swallowed hard, betraying the passion waiting to be expressed. His other hand came up to reverently touch the length of her hair as it lay on one shoulder.

By way of answer, Margaret reached behind him and locked the bedroom door. "I do not wish to wait," she said, and Thornton quickly realized that was all the invitation he needed.

Chapter Fifteen

The Dawning Light

Light entered slowly the next morning, creeping cautiously under and around the heavy muslin curtains as if, like a living person, it hesitated to disturb the newlywed couple. But eventually it lightly touched their faces and woke them to the first full day of their married life.

Margaret stirred first, surprised to discover that awakening in her husband's arms could feel so natural. She did not need to open her eyes to feel cocooned next to him, to savor the warmth and safety of his embrace. Had John really loved her last night with the vital, physical force she remembered, or had it all been an astonishing dream? If she could see his face again perhaps she could convince herself of the strength of her memory. She began to turn towards him, but his arms tightening around her prevented the action.

"Where are you going, Margaret?" Thornton's voice was a bare murmur in her ear.

"Nowhere, without you," she answered. "I just want to look at you."

His arms loosened slightly and she faced him fully, raising one hand to caress the dark hair she had admired so often, memorizing his features from this new angle. Thornton's eyes closed to savor her touch more completely.

"I believe I am going to enjoy being married to you," he said after a moment with his eyes still closed, his tone indulgent and teasing. "I wonder that we did not marry before now."

"You did try to marry me quite a while ago." Margaret was perfectly willing to tease him in return. "If only I had been more cooperative!"

Thornton opened his eyes to look at her more fully. "You have nothing to recriminate yourself for, my love. Neither of us really understood the other just then. We both had a great deal to learn of each other's characters in order to love each other as we ought. But everything is now as it should be, and that is all that matters."

Margaret accepted his affectionate kiss for a minute before laying her head back on his shoulder with a contented sigh. "John, may I ask you a question?"

"Of course, my love; anything."

"Why did you never marry before now? I know it was not for lack of opportunity."

"Who told you that, love?"

"Your mother made it clear to me that you were pursued by many eligible young ladies, and I have no trouble believing it."

Thornton smiled slightly. "I never had time to fall in love. I was too busy, too preoccupied with the mill."

"But you were not too busy to fall in love with *me*, so how did your schedule change so abruptly?"

"It did not. I had no more time to fall in love with you than I did with anyone else, but you gave me no choice in the matter."

"No choice!"

"I had no choice but to love you after I had spent so much time in company with you and your father and learned to appreciate your generous heart, and especially no choice after the night of our dinner party. I had feelings for you before then, but that was when I could no longer deny to myself what they were."

"The same night when I spoke my beliefs so strongly, and humiliated myself and half the company?" Margaret asked, looking equal parts doubt and delight.

"The night when you refused to be intimidated by anyone present, and spoke your mind strongly but compassionately, betraying your gracious spirit," Thornton corrected her.

"So you were won over by my mind and my heart."

"And your own natural form, which is so beautiful to me," her husband added, kissing her yet again. After a minute he asked, "When did you know that you loved *me*?"

"I have no idea. There was no particular day which I can remember in the same way that you can. I felt it for some time before I could put it into words in my mind. But after my father died, when I came to give you his book of Plato, I knew that I did not want to leave Milton at all because it would mean leaving you!"

"Is that how you were feeling?" Thornton asked, musing gently on the memory. "I wish I had known. I could barely stand to watch you go. It felt as though my very soul was being rent apart, having you taken from me like that."

"When I gave you father's book there was a moment when I thought that you felt some regret at my leaving--but a moment later you face hardened and you turned away. I believed then that I could never change your opinion of me, and that I would never see you again."

"You mistook my feelings entirely, my dearest. I only turned away to avoid betraying the depths of my feelings for you, believing *you* would never care for *me*. When you drove away that day, I was watching after you as long as I could, hoping against hope that you might give me any kind of sign that you cared for me. I watched until you rounded the corner, longing to see you look back at me just once."

"And what would you have done if I had?"

"I don't know." He thought for a moment. "Run out and fallen to my knees in the snow, begging you to stay, I suppose."

"Dear me, how scandalous that would have been!" Margaret said, smiling at the thought. "I am glad not to have seen you driven to such desperate measures."

"No measure would have been too desperate, if it meant being with you," Thornton said, caressing her gently, and Margaret's memories of the night before were soon awash in an even greater experience.

Chapter Sixteen

Day of Reckoning

It was some time later when Thornton and Margaret awoke again, aroused by the cautious steps of the servants in the rooms below. Thornton sighed regretfully. "I am sorry to say that we must rise, my love. There is a great deal to be accomplished today."

"Yes, I know. The mills."

"Indeed. Today will be a day of reckoning, I fear. Daughtry, Watson's foreman, will be here to call on me shortly. I asked him to come to me here rather than at Hayleigh Mills so that we might discuss the state of the mill freely, with no danger of being listened in on by the workers. I have no idea what he might tell me--he may know nothing or he may know a great deal. After I find that out I suppose I will have to go to Watson's office and see what I can discover for myself about his affairs."

"And I will go to the parsonage and take my turn sitting with Watson," Margaret told him. "Fanny and your mother ought to have a chance to leave the sickroom for a little while." Thornton agreed heartily with her plan, and so they rose and prepared for the day.

When they arrived downstairs for breakfast they found that a message had already arrived from Hannah, saying that Watson had improved slightly overnight. His color was better, his breathing was not as shallow, and he had opened his eyes briefly in response to Fanny's voice. Dr. Donaldson was due to call on his patient in a short while. Assuming that both Fanny and Hannah would wish to be present when the doctor arrived, Margaret took her time in readying herself to go to them. Thus she was still at home when Geoffrey Daughtry was announced into the parlor to meet her husband.

Daughtry was a well-dressed, middle-aged man whose eyes concealed a tension betrayed by his firmly set mouth and the hat clenched in his hands. He politely extended his congratulations to Thornton on his recent marriage and then quickly asked if he had any further news of Watson's condition.

"There has apparently been some improvement, for which we are grateful, but there is a long ways to go yet. If you will take a seat we can begin to discuss the status of the mill at this time."

Daughtry sat and Thornton called for tea, but the beverage had not been served before the door was opened again, this time to admit Slickson, the mill owner who had first rejected Thornton for employment. He had just arrived at the Thornton's and requested the favor of an audience. Since both men were presumably there to speak on the same subject, Thornton saw no reason not to admit him and ask him to likewise be seated. But his greeting was cool, and the welcome he gave Slickson was not as friendly as the welcome he had given Daughtry.

"I suppose you are here in regards to Watson's collapse," he began, speaking to Slickson in a business-like tone while eyeing him distrustfully. "He has apparently improved slightly since yesterday; however, I can assure you that he will not be in any condition to tend to business for some time. I believe he has no heirs besides my sister, who knows nothing of business." Here he stopped and looked questioningly at Daughtry, who nodded. "Therefore, it is my responsibility to see to Watson's business affairs until he can take them over again himself. I claim this right and duty as Watson's brother."

Slickson frowned but made no response. Daughtry nodded, apparently amenable to the idea, but his lips tightened in concern. Thornton looked down at the list of items he had prepared to discuss. "What are your immediate needs? How long will Hayleigh Mills be able to operate without an infusion of cash? Do you know if the payroll is safe?"

"I don't know," Daughtry told him, not trying to conceal his ignorance. "Mr. Watson kept a sharp eye on all his business matters and left very little to me off of the floor. All I can tell you now is that the mill is open today."

"I was afraid that might be all you could tell me," Thornton replied. "I suppose you have the keys to Watson's office? I will need to go in and examine his books as soon as possible. It is no good having his men work if there is no means to pay them."

"Mr. Watson has a clerk, a young man who will probably be able to help you with the ledgers," Daughtry told him. "I have already sent a messenger for him, and he should arrive at the mill later today."

"Very good; I thank you. I am counting on your support during this time of transition. I will rely on you to manage matters just as you would if Watson were here."

"You may depend upon it, sir," Daughtry replied strongly, and Thornton felt relieved by his steady manner. Daughtry was anxious, as was only right under the circumstances, but he seemed ready to face whatever difficulties might be ahead.

At this point Slickson made an impatient noise in his throat, and both of the other men turned to look at him. Thornton raised one eyebrow, making no effort to conceal the dislike he was feeling for the man, but Slickson did not hesitate.

"Thornton, we have urgent business to discuss."

"We are discussing it now," Thornton answered coolly. "Nothing is more urgent than safeguarding my sister's well-being by caring for her husband's interests."

"You know what I mean. Your business and mine coincide. I must have a look at Watson's books as well."

"I am sorry, Slickson," Thornton replied sternly. "You have mistaken me for one of your employees. I am not obligated to share any information with you."

"Deuce take it all!" Slickson exploded. "It's *my* money invested with Watson in this lunatic scheme of his! How he talked me into it I shall never know. But I came here today as soon as I heard how he collapsed over the loss of the speculation. I need to know the state of his affairs, to understand how much I have lost. I need to look at his books!"

"All will be carried out in good order!" Thornton said angrily. "I am a magistrate, after all; it is my duty to see that the law is obeyed, and I will carry it out! I will not give you any information which I do not give the other investors."

"The other masters will be calling on you, too, Thornton, sooner or later. You cannot ignore all of us together."

Thornton recalled Watson's request to convey his regrets to the other masters and winced inwardly. How far had their own property become entangled with this sorry business? "How bad is it, Slickson?" he asked in a low voice, unblinking. "Did the other investors pledge their personal property as well?"

Slickson looked down briefly, shuffling his feet uncomfortably. "They did."

"And are you all ruined, Slickson?" Thornton demanded, leaning forward in his chair. "Will any of your businesses be able to go on?"

Slickson slumped back in his seat and wiped his forehead with his kerchief, much as Watson had done in the church. "I am ruined, Thornton, ruined beyond all hope of redemption. I cannot speak for the others, but my property is certainly gone."

"Then why are you here?" Thornton asked, not bothering to cover his disdain for the man. "What is it that you want from me?"

Slickson placed his elbows on Thornton's desk, letting his head fall into his hands while he pressed against them with his forehead, the very picture of wretchedness. "If I could just have a little time . . . I still have orders to fill, with promises of more orders on the way. My equipment is good, and I have supplies and labor on hand. I can dig myself out of this hole with just a little time. Just a few months, and I could begin to be solvent again."

"What do you imagine *I* can do?" Thornton asked, feeling a small measure of pity despite himself. The man's dejection and self-loathing were almost palpable. "I do not own your debts, as you well know."

Slickson looked up at Thornton, his eyes bright with desperation. "But they will listen to you," he said hoarsely. "You are respected in this town. If you could convince our creditors to wait, to let them know that if they are patient, they will have their money . . . "

"And why do you think they will listen to me?" Thornton scoffed. "The bankers gave *me* no relief when I asked them for it!"

"Then try a different tactic. You have married an heiress; surely you can afford to take up our debts yourself, and give us a chance to make good on our losses without demanding immediate repayment. If you do not, the whole town of Milton will suffer." Neither man noticed that Margaret had entered the room, and now she stood quietly in the corner, listening.

"Now you speak as a mad man." Thornton shook his head in disbelief. "I did not marry my wife in order to use her money in a speculation, and even if I were minded to use it that way, there is not enough. I cannot be your salvation; it sounds like no one can."

"You have to help us, Thornton!"

"My wife's money will not be used to rescue people from their own wild schemes. If that is your goal is coming here today, I will bid you good day."

"But you do not understand, Thornton. I am not thinking only of myself, or even of the other investors. The people in this town are desperate. If they hear that half the mills in this town are going to close, then they will burn half of Milton along with them! They will have nothing to lose!"

"No!" Margaret exclaimed, unable to keep silent any longer. She stepped forward to face the startled men. "You do them wrong! I do not believe they would be so foolhardy!"

"Do you not, Mrs. Thornton? Then let me tell you something," said Slickson, speaking earnestly. "There is an anger on the streets today, an anger growing by the minute, and it will only get worse from here on out. Today, walking here, I could feel the eyes of workers following my every step; when the dire situation becomes more fully known, when the first mill has to shut its doors, it may be worth my life to step foot out of doors."

"I do not believe that," Margaret said emphatically.

"Nor do I," Thornton echoed. He looked questioningly at Daughtry, who shook his head.

"He is exaggerating. There is anger, but I don't believe there will be violence."

"Remember the strike, Thornton! Remember the day of the riot! We all thought there would be little danger then, either, and yet look what happened," Slickson countered, and saw at once that his comment had hit the mark. Thornton sat back in his chair to consider Slickson's words more fully.

It would be easy to dismiss Slickson's warning as the desperate maneuvers of a bankrupted businessman trying to preserve his concerns at any cost--and yet, there was also Higgins. Higgins had mentioned on Sunday, just two days ago, that the mood of the town was desperate. He had even gone so far as to predict that riots might occur if word came out that the masters of the town were ruined, but at the time Thornton had disregarded the warning, believing as he did that Watson and the others were safe. But now that that had turned out not to be the case, Thornton realized that there might be a solid basis for Slickson's predictions.

But it was still no good. He shook his head as if to clear it. "I hope you are wrong, Slickson, but even if you are right there is nothing I can do about it. I do not have the means, even with my wife's fortune, to purchase your debts, nor would I care to do so."

"But the bankers--could you not put in a word for us, to tell them that if they are patient, they are sure to be repaid?"

"I cannot give them any reassurance which I do not have myself. They would have to be convinced of your eventual solvency on their own, and I do not know how they could be convinced of that."

Margaret had been silently listening for several minutes, but now she spoke again, her voice quiet but compelling.

"Mr. Slickson, do you know how many mills are in danger? How many masters bought into the speculation?"

Slickson answered wearily, with seeming hopelessness. "It was a dozen, ma'am. A dozen mills that will end up shuttered because of our foolishness."

"And how many masters stayed out of the scheme? How many are left untouched?"

"Another dozen, ma'am, counting your husband here."

Margaret mulled this over in her head for a moment, and then spoke to her husband. "John, I have an idea which may be able to answer the needs of the creditors, the people of Milton, and even the masters themselves. I hope you will allow me speak of it here."

Wordlessly John nodded, his face a study in confusion, and without further delay Margaret began to explain.

Chapter Seventeen

A Solid Foundation

The various masters of Milton convened at Marlborough Mills early that afternoon, alerted by runners commissioned by both Thornton and Slickson. Many of the masters brought their own clerks with them, each carrying detailed records of the investments made, the returns realized, and the debts yet to be paid. Other masters, the ones who had not invested with Watson, brought only themselves and a keen sense of curiosity. As they had not been involved with the speculation, why would Thornton desire their presence? But they came anyway, knowing that what happened with the other less fortunate businesses in town would affect them all. The whole group stood restlessly on the factory floor, speaking amongst themselves in hushed voices while they waited to see what would happen next and why they had been summoned.

In the factory office Thornton, Margaret and Slickson were all gathered around Thornton's desk, looking over the details of the plan which Margaret had first communicated and which Thornton had carefully committed to paper. Watson's ledgers, retrieved from Hayleigh Mills, were arrayed on one side of the desk and guarded diligently by Daughtry, who looked on worriedly as first Slickson and then Thornton checked figures on their papers again and again, comparing them to entries from one ledger or another. Margaret watched in silence. Finally Thornton lifted his head and spoke confidently. "It will work."

"It will have to work. We have no other choice," Slickson replied, but Thornton shook his head.

"Merely wishing for a scheme to be successful does not mean that it will be. That kind of thinking is what got us into this position to begin with. The reorganization will work, not because we want it to, but because it has a solid foundation of cooperation based on mutual concerns. Well done, my love," he added, with a special smile just for Margaret.

"You added to my idea considerably," she told him.

"Slickson and I merely fleshed out the details. The foundation and framework were entirely yours."

"You will need to present the proposal in its entirety to the other masters, and to the investors," Slickson told Thornton, ignoring their exchange. "I will lend my full support, but if it comes from you it is likely to be better received, and to have a better chance of being accepted by all concerned."

There was a light rap on the office door and a thin, graying man in a finely tailored suit entered. Margaret recognized him as Miles Latimer, the banker who had been Thornton's liaison with the bank in the past, and whose daughter Amy had attended Fanny and Watson's wedding with Thornton. "I understand you desire my presence on a matter of some urgency, Thornton."

"Indeed. You already know Slickson, here, and please allow me to introduce my wife, Margaret Thornton, formerly Margaret Hale, and Mr. Daughtry, the foreman of Hayleigh Mills."

Latimer nodded courteously at Daughtry and offered his congratulations to Margaret. Then he spoke to Thornton. "I presume you have gathered everyone here to discuss the end of the speculation. A sorry business indeed. The bank will be grievously injured by the failure of this loan."

"Yes, well, that is why I called you here. Margaret has devised a plan which will be of benefit to us all. I want you to hear it."

"Mrs. Thornton devised a plan?" Latimer repeated skeptically.

"You *will* allow her to explain." There was a compelling tone in Thornton's voice and in his eyes which few men ever denied, and after a moment Latimer seated himself and nodded at her to proceed. Margaret began at once.

"My idea is based on the presumption that all of the businesses involved with the speculation are fundamentally sound. All of them have orders to fill, all of them have at least some material on hand, all of them have the necessary machinery and labor immediately available. What they lack more than anything is money to pay their workers, yet that is what they need in order to continue operations and bring in more income in order to pay their loans. Those mills must be allowed to operate."

"Easier said than done," Latimer said impatiently.

"What I propose is a sort of reorganization of the speculation. Instead of declaring it totally bankrupt, we will form a new concern--"

"A trust," Thornton supplied.

"Yes, a trust whose purpose is to gather all the existing orders together in one and oversee their fulfillment. The money to pay these workers will come from the masters who are still solvent, along with an investment of my own. The payments received will go first to reducing the debt owed to the bank, next to the landlords involved with each mill, and then to a small payment which will be made to each of the investors, both the solvent and the insolvent. Once the entire debt is paid in full, the new corporation will dissolve."

"For the time being, the masters who did not invest with Watson will manufacture only as part of the trust. They will invest, in a way, but in a manner which will benefit us all," added Thornton. "It will be almost as though all the mills of Milton are acting as part of the same enterprise."

Latimer was listening closely. "What makes you think the other masters would go along with this? And why would any payment at all go to the bankrupt investors? They are bankrupt, after all; the very word means they ought to expect nothing."

"The small amount they will receive will be used to allow them to remain in their homes, which ought to satisfy them," Margaret explained. "There are a dozen bankrupt mills, each with at least several hundred employees. We will need almost all of them in order to fulfill the existing orders, and there will not be enough room for their shifts at the remaining mills. They will have to continue to work in their own mills, and for that we will need the cooperation of those masters."

Latimer frowned in concentration. "I begin to see. And you will need the cooperation of all of their landlords as well, hence the payments to them."

"Indeed. This plan will depend on everyone cooperating, and it will buy everyone the time they need in order for the debt to be repaid."

"But are there enough orders pending to keep all the mill employees working? For how long? And what will happen when those orders are fulfilled?"

"New orders will be coming in," Thornton assured him, "as soon as our buyers realize that we still have the ability to fulfill them. If we go on producing cotton products just as before, they will have no reason not to continue to purchase from us. They will merely be doing business with all of us, under a different name."

"I can see how this might work," Latimer said, hesitantly, "but it is still a risk."

"All business is risk. At least this risk will not be based on the outcome of a war in South America! How could you have allowed such a loan to go forward, Latimer?" Thornton demanded.

"It was against my better judgment," Latimer admitted, "but the underwriters did not consult me. And bankers are as greedy as any other men."

"Greed is what puts women and children out on the streets,"

Margaret told him, speaking with some asperity. "What we mean to accomplish here is to protect as many of them as possible."

"I am still not sure if I like this plan," Latimer said slowly, still considering it carefully. "What about the personal property pledged to us as security? The underwriters will insist on having it."

"And they can still have it, at least some of it," Margaret said persuasively. "Possessions not needed for daily living by the bankrupt investors will be surrendered to the new trust. What they need for daily life will remain with them. Together with their allowance, it ought to be enough to maintain a certain standard of living."

"But the bank is still bound to lose some income from this," Latimer said, shaking his head. "No, I am sorry. I cannot allow that."

"We will all lose some income," Thornton responded. He had waited for this moment to present this part of the plan, so that Latimer would not reject it out of hand. "For this to work everyone will have to come together and act as one. The other mill owners will have to agree to forego manufacturing under their own name for some time, so that they do not compete with the trust which we will establish. The landlords will have to agree to lower rents. The bankrupt investors will still have to surrender some property. But it will be much better than all of us going down together, do you not agree? Wouldn't the bank prefer the repayment of a large percentage of its money rather than demanding every penny, if the alternative is a total loss?"

"So you will ask the bank to forgive a percentage of the debt, in order to avoid a total collapse?" Latimer looked at Thornton with a keen, appraising look.

Thornton nodded. "They will have to, in order for this plan to work. That is the final piece of the plan."

"And it makes sense," Margaret could not help adding. "They knew how risky the speculation was, and yet they allowed it to proceed anyway."

Latimer smiled grimly at her. "I do not disagree with you."

He stood from his chair and walked restlessly around the room for a minute, his hand ruffling up his beard, until he finally came to stand before Thornton. "Who will convince the solvent masters to throw in their lot with the rest of us?"

"I will speak to them myself," Thornton answered, "and make them see that this is the only way to save Milton."

"But will they listen to you?"

Slickson fairly snorted at this point. "Latimer, Thornton is the one man in this town to whom they *will* listen. He is the only man who has money invested in the plan already who is willing to put *more* into it in order to keep it from collapsing."

Latimer looked at Thornton in confusion. "More! But you did not invest."

"I did not, but my wife's godfather did. The ledgers here show that most of his money was regained, and he did not pledge any of his personal property before signing it all over to Margaret. Thus although she did lose some money most of her inheritance is safe, and she is willing to invest a sizable proportion of it into the trust."

"If Thornton says they should throw their lot in with the trust, you may be sure they'll do it," Slickson said decisively. "As for the bankrupt investors, I will speak with them. Thornton's plan is the most generous outcome they can possibly expect. They'll go along with it rather than face complete ruin."

Latimer drummed his fingers on the desk for a moment as he stared absently into space, apparently lost in thought. Finally he said, "I have known you for many years, Thornton, and I believe you know of what you speak. Show me all the figures which you have worked up. I need to know exactly how much cash this trust would have in hand, what the payroll would be, how many orders are waiting to be filled, and a dozen other details. I need to know all the particulars, Thornton! If you can convince me, then I will do my best to convince the underwriters."

Thornton smiled, the triumphant look of a man who knows that a well-laid plan is coming together. "Slickson, please go out on the floor and bring in the other investors, five at a time. Let us see what we have to work with."

Chapter Eighteen

A Matter of Trust

In the end all parties agreed to the plan, the bankrupt investors with a mixture of relief and resignation and the solvent masters with considerably less enthusiasm. Several of the latter group made the objection that they should not be penalized for their prudence by having their profits restricted as much as Margaret's plan contemplated, a point with which both the Thorntons found it difficult to argue. Gradually it was agreed that their share of the income realized would exceed the share paid to the other group by a certain percentage, and with that change made, the details came together. Latimer began to put more faith in the plan as he followed Thornton's presentation of it multiple times, occasionally proposing small modifications of his own which went a long ways towards ensuring everyone's cooperation. By the end of the day Thornton had a solid agreement written down and a signature of commitment from every person concerned except for Latimer, who could not do so without speaking to the underwriters first. But even he was now speaking in terms of when they would give their approval to the reorganization, rather than if they would agree at all.

"The final item which the underwriters will need to know before giving their approval is the name of the person who will administer the trust," Latimer said as he finished writing out his copious notes for presentation the next day. "Can I tell them that it will be you, Thornton? No one else will do. You would draw a salary appropriate for the trustee of a concern of this size, of course, until the trust is dissolved."

"I, the trustee?" Thornton echoed. It made sense that he should be the one to oversee the working out of the practical details of the trust, but until this moment he had been too preoccupied with securing everyone's agreement to think that far ahead.

"It will have to be you," Latimer replied, regarding Thornton seriously. "No other business man in this town commands the respect that you do, and you will be seen as the plan's architect--begging your pardon, ma'am," he added apologetically to Margaret, who nodded briefly in acknowledgement.

"It matters not who gets the credit, so long as the plan works," she said.

"*I* will not accept anyone else as the trustee," Slickson said in an impatient tone. "Say that you will take the position and let us be done with it."

How the tables had turned! Thornton was suddenly overcome by the weight of the responsibility being thrust upon him. The fate of the town might well ride on his ability to guide this enterprise through to fulfillment. If he failed, many would suffer, but if he succeeded, his place as one of the most prominent leaders of the town would be assured for any number of years. Instinctively he sought out Margaret's face, seeking the reassurance he needed.

She sensed his new anxiety. "You will not be alone," she said with a certain quiet pride, and Thornton felt warmth surge through him. He looked at Slickson next, his expression stern.

"You rejected me as unsuitable when I came to you for a job. You told me that I was not a man of vision, that I did not pursue opportunities when they became available and that I was not willing to take the necessary risks of business."

Slickson flushed and opened his mouth to speak, but Thornton cut him off. "Never mind. I think I know what you would say next, and I will not be so mean as to insist on hearing the words. For the sake of this town and our fellow business owners, I will take the position."

"You are a good man, Thornton," Slickson said with a look that apologized for everything. He shook his hand firmly, and Daughtry and Latimer repeated the action. Thornton looked at his watch.

"And now it is past time for us to check on my mother, Fanny and Watson," he said, the tedium of the day beginning to catch up to him, and Margaret agreed with him. With a sigh of relief he and Margaret bade the gentlemen farewell and they all made their way out of the office doors and down the stairs into the main workroom. A handful of investors still remained, speaking quietly among themselves, and it was necessary to take leave of them as well before Thornton and Margaret could make their way to the door. But at last they did gain the door of the factory, only to be stopped short by the sharp odor of smoke and a distant orange glow in the twilight of the northeastern sky, a dark plume beginning to rise steadily and ominously.

"What is that, John?" Margaret asked in alarm, clinging to his arm, while the others inside the mill began to follow them outside. "I thought I noticed an odd odor when we were inside, but I paid it no attention. Is that a building on fire?"

Thornton could only stand mesmerized, staring in disbelief towards the scene he knew must be unfolding. Passersby on the street, business men and workers alike, were stopping to look, to point, and to exclaim.

Daughtry left the mill last and pushed impatiently to the front of the small gathering crowd. "My god, it's Hamper's mill!" he exclaimed. "They've set it ablaze!"

Margaret rounded on him. "You do not know that!"

"That is Hamper's mill, ma'am, and I know what the workers have threatened in the past! The fire company--we must rouse the fire brigade!"

"If we can see it from here, then the fire brigade must already know about it," Thornton replied, his mind racing to take in this newest occurrence. He laid a hand protectively on his wife's shoulder. "Margaret, I need to go see for myself what is happening. Go inside the house and stay there until I return."

"I will not!" Margaret looked at him indignantly. "I will go wherever you go!"

"I will not put you in danger. If they have set Hamper's ablaze there's no telling what else they might do. I want you to be safe."

"And I want the same for you, but you will still go towards the danger regardless, won't you?"

Thornton's eyes flared. "This is different! You are my responsibility now, and I will protect you to the best of my ability! You must go inside the house and keep order while I go with the men to see what can be done!"

"I *will* go with you," Margaret insisted, prepared to fight for what she wanted, but the budding argument was abruptly cut off by the arrival of Nicholas Higgins in the yard, riding at a run into the mill yard on the back of a small roan. The horse was bareback, and he pulled the animal up and fairly slid off of it, all in one motion.

"They've set Hamper's mill ablaze," he told them breathlessly, "and there's an angry mob wanting to do more damage than that. None of you masters should be on the street right now."

"Did the workers truly set the fire on purpose?" Margaret asked him, her eyes wide with horror, and Nicholas nodded.

"Saw it with my own eyes. I was there, trying to talk some sense into them, when I saw a man break a window and throw a torch in, and then I ran for my life. That cotton burns hot and fast. There'll be nothing left of the mill in an hour!"

"God save us all if that fire spreads!" Daughtry exclaimed. "Hayleigh Mills is only a half mile from Hamper's!"

"Was there anyone in Hamper's?" Thornton demanded of Nicholas. "Are there any lives lost?"

"No, master, not as far as I know. They had been hearing rumors all day that the mill would not open tomorrow, and that they wouldn't be paid for today either. Soon as they left their shifts they started yelling and carrying on so that it caught my attention and I went to see what was happening, and then the torch went through the window. After that I came here as fast as I could to let you know. I'm telling you, you and the other masters need to get inside somewhere before any of that angry mob decides to come this way."

"Fools, to destroy their only means of livelihood!" Slickson said bitterly. "How do they think they will ever work, if the mill is gone? We need to call the soldiers on them."

"They don't know, John," said Margaret in a low, urgent voice, her hand clutching his arm. "The workers don't know what was accomplished here today, and that they will have jobs tomorrow. They think there is nothing left to save. Someone has to tell them that their fears are groundless."

"You are right; someone will have to inform them. I suppose it will be me," he said in frustration, running an impatient hand through his hair. Would this awful sequence of events never end? How many momentous events could be packed into such a short period of time? "Higgins, where are they? Can you take me to them?"

Higgins' mouth dropped open almost comically. "Are you out of your mind, master? I came here to get you away from them, not to have you run straight to them!"

"Will they listen to me, if I tell them their fears are needless?"

"I don't know if they will listen to anyone, they're that angry! But if they *were* to listen to anyone, it would be you."

"Then take me to them at once. I have my duty. Margaret, stay here."

By way of response Margaret looked fiercely at her husband, her expression saying more than words ever could. Thornton hesitated. "You will come regardless of anything I say, won't you?" Their gazes battled each other for another few moments, and then Thornton smiled as he boldly exclaimed, "God, how I love you!" He briefly kissed her, conceding defeat, and then he, Margaret, and Higgins all swiftly boarded the Thornton carriage together.

Chapter Nineteen

Stopping the Fire

The Thornton carriage traveled as rapidly as it dared through the streets of Milton, passing growing numbers of those who were coming outside their homes or businesses to point at the rising plume of smoke and conjecture as to its source. Other carriages sped past them in the opposite direction, their passengers wide eyed as they urged their drivers to hurry on, but their own carriage made straight for the danger. Abruptly Higgins rapped on the roof to signal the driver, then leaned out and called up to direct him to Hayleigh Mills. The carriage resumed its pace.

"Going to Hamper's will do us no good," Higgins told the others when he was fully inside again. "It's as good as gone already, and the fire brigade wouldn't let us near anyways. If there's more mischief to be carried out it'll be done at Hayleigh, seeing as it's so close."

Neither John nor Margaret could answer, for as they changed direction slightly, turning down a smaller side street, they could begin to see from the carriage window the height of the flames from Hamper's, reaching over the tops of the smaller buildings before it. There were no more curious observers standing on the street. The smell of smoke increased and a great roaring sound began to press on their ears, mixed with the distant cries of men and the sounds of breaking glass. Though they were still a handful of blocks away from the conflagration, Margaret fancied she could begin to feel its heat seeping through the very carriage itself. Instinctively she shrank back from the carriage walls, but her husband and Higgins were leaning forward to see as much as possible out of the small window.

The carriage stopped again, this time of its own accord, and the driver came hurriedly around to them. "I dare not go closer, sir," he told

Thornton. "Besides the fire there's the crowd just up ahead."

"What crowd?" Thornton asked. "What are they doing?"

"A bit of a mob. See for yourself."

Thornton peered out the window, then jumped out and held his hand out to Margaret. "Margaret, stay as close to me as possible. There's an ugly group of men up there. Do not allow even an inch to separate us. Higgins, you stay close too." He pulled her to his side and began to stride rapidly towards the crowd which was barely visible in the haze caused by the smoke blocking the waning sun overhead.

Despite Thornton's words, it was a crowd comprised of both men and women who came into Margaret's view as she hurried next to her husband. They had apparently just come from Hamper's and were now walking south en masse towards the looming iron gate of Hayleigh Mills, visible about three blocks ahead. All was noisy confusion in the premature dusk caused by the cloud of smoke now casting an eerie shadow on all below. As the crowd passed through the intersection and streamed down the street, towards Margaret's right, she could hear their words being called out like a battle cry. "To Hayleigh! Put the torch there too! Let Watson feel what it means to be out on the street! Down with Hamper! Down with Watson! Cut all the masters down to size!"

Into this stream of angry humanity Thornton rushed, with Margaret just behind him and Higgins bringing up the rear. In just a few moments, by pushing this way and that and squeezing through openings in the men at the front of the crowd, they were able to reach the front. This was their most dangerous moment. They must break in front of the mob and stop the headlong march towards madness, convincing them to turn aside for their own good and the good of the town, all without sounding as though they were taking part in any scheme against the workers. Fortune favored the interlopers here, for the street narrowed slightly to allow for a great oversized counting house on one side, and when the three had turned to face the marchers and stop them in their tracks there was little room to go past on either side. There they stood, Thornton, Margaret, and Higgins all in a line, and did not move.

"Turn aside from this mischief of yours!" Higgins cried, his voice carrying loudly on the street, despite the presence of so many people. "I say turn aside! There's no need for this foolishness!"

The crowd did not even slow down. "Out of our way, Higgins!" yelled one of the advancing men in response. "Out of our way, or be dragged along with us!" He made as if to step past the little group, but without a word Higgins stepped in front of him, blocking his path, sending a message with no words by the fists clenched at his sides. The man stopped in his tracks. Behind him the crowd slowed, then began to mass together like a wave about to crash on a shore.

"You must stop!" Thornton cried, stepping up to stand at Higgins' side. "You can save your jobs and your homes if you don't burn Milton down first!" Behind them, Margaret stood silent and attentive, listening carefully but not yet willing to speak.

Another man, tall and burly, stepped forward with a torch held tightly in his right hand. The light from the torch illuminated weirdly on his cragged face as he spoke. "Are you here as a magistrate, Thornton, to arrest us? Or as a master, to protect your friends? Either way step aside, or we will go right through you!"

"I am here as a man!" Thornton told him, speaking as loudly as he could, "a fellow citizen of Milton, to turn you away from actions you will regret tomorrow. There is no hope for you if you continue in this mad way, but if you will listen to reason we can all survive this disaster." He folded his arms as he had on the day of the riot and stood defiantly.

The crowd had stopped their yelling in order to hear this exchange, and now a second man stepped roughly to the front, his manner dark and disapproving. "I don't believe you. Masters is always out to protect their own."

"That is not true," Higgins told him, his voice quieter now but still ringing clearly. "There's at least one good man among them, and his name is John Thornton. You'll listen to what he says or you'll answer to me."

"He's here to tell us what we want to hear!"

"I am here to give you a voice in your own future!" Thornton answered. "Will you not hear the plan we devised? It was my wife's idea--surely you do not doubt *her* intentions!"

"Your wife!"

The mention of Margaret seemed to throw the group into confusion, and Margaret took advantage of the moment to step proudly next to her husband, though she shook inwardly. "Miss Hale?" one of the crowd finally asked in disbelief, and Margaret raised her chin as she looked back at them.

"I am Margaret Thornton now, and I came here with my husband," she glanced up at him as she spoke, "to tell you not to do this terrible thing. Go home. I know you are frightened, that you wonder if you will be left to be thrown out on the street or starve. But you will be paid for the work you did today, and if you leave the other mills alone, I can promise you will still have work tomorrow."

"You can't promise us that!" scoffed the man who appeared to be the leader of the group, at least for the moment, but he tilted his head slightly as though considering her words. "Nobody can promise us anything!"

"I can!" Thornton contradicted him. "The masters and bankers have come together for the good of the town. If you will stop your people right now, you can come to Marlborough Mills tomorrow and find out what has been agreed upon to protect everyone."

"What *you* have agreed upon!" still another marcher sneered, seeming angrier than the first two. "*The masters and bankers* have come together! There's some deal been made, no doubt, between the lot of you, but us workers have had no part in it. We've no say in any agreement, not now or ever, and it's us as always pay the price when things go wrong!"

"Is this your solution?" Margaret stepped forward boldly, causing her husband's eyes to widen, but he made no move to stop her. "Do you really wish to destroy the only way you have of earning income? Burning the mills serves no one, and who is to say where it will stop? The soldiers are sure to be called on to deal with you. You are not thinking clearly. Everybody should go home now, while they can still do so safely, and see what tomorrow will bring."

The crowd stood uncertainly, not knowing what to say or where to go. Some looked as if they wanted to continue forward, but with Higgins, a known union leader, and Thornton, the man who had broken the strike, both standing in the way they were hesitant to press their point. Then too, Margaret was known to many of them by reputation, and they were reluctant to march on any woman. The leader of the group glanced to either side of him, at the eager, angry faces mixed with the more doubtful looks, and then back at Thornton again. "Tell us now about this plan you've made. Why should we believe it'll be anything that will benefit us?"

"Because the other masters will step in to help with the debt of those who are bankrupt, and all will work together instead of working against each other. Everyone concerned has agreed to reduce their profits and put the needs of the town first!"

"*That's* your angle, then!" cried the surly man who had spoken earlier. "You want us to give up our wages to help the masters! We'll take a cut to put money back in their pockets!" The crowd behind him, hearing his words, began to roar, but Margaret spoke out again, stepping still closer to the mob.

"No! You'll not lose a shilling! That was a part of the plan all along!"

At this, even Thornton turned his head to look at his wife in surprise, and the crowd stopped yelling as all eyes fixed on her.

"The plan we devised protects the workers most of all! The masters and banks and landlords will all have to yield some of their profits for this to work, but they have agreed to do so in order to avoid losing everything they have. But not so with you! The workers *have* nothing to give up! Nothing will be required of you except to go on working as you have. It is not fair that you are always the ones who suffer for the mistakes of others. Your wages will stay exactly as they are today, with no reductions at all--unless there is no mill left for you to work in!"

The eyes of the men in front of her narrowed as they considered her words, and their expressions became more and more perplexed. "We need not be enemies in this," she finished. "Go home tonight, and send a delegation to Marlborough Mills tomorrow morning. You will hear the plan in its entirety then, and I promise you, it will work! I have pledged my own fortune to it!"

"I can vouch for the lady." Higgins added his support to Margaret. "She means what she says. We will all have jobs."

The leader who had first spoken remained silent for a moment, the torch remaining uncertainly in his grasp. With his free hand he wiped a sleeve across his eyes as if to help himself see more clearly. "Hamper's is gone," he said, his despair plain. "There'll be no more jobs for those of us who worked there."

"But Marlborough Mills is going to open again," Thornton told him. "And any man who was at Hamper's and makes no mischief this night can have a place with me."

The man looked back Thornton warily, almost hungrily. "You'd give all of us work? All of us who were at Hamper's today?"

"All but the man who first torched the place," Thornton confirmed. "I won't make room for *him*. But the rest of you can take work with me if

Higgins vouches for you."

There was silence for a moment. The three stood facing the crowd together, waiting for someone to make the first move, and then the leader at the front dipped his torch. He sank the flaming end of it into the damp earth at his feet, and the smoke rose like a sign of surrender. "If Higgins vouches for you and this plan of yours, that's good enough for me. I have a family to support. If you'll have me I'll take your work, and be glad of it."

"You'll be more than welcome," Thornton told him, extending a hand to shake, but he kept his gaze cool and his eyes alert. The danger was not yet over.

"Well *I'm* not going to Marlborough Mills tomorrow," announced the surly man to his right. "I'm going to Hayleigh Mills right now, to make a grand bonfire out of everything Watson left behind." He roughly pushed his comrades aside and began to move again, making straight for Thornton, who dropped his arms and stood to his full height, awaiting the onslaught. But before he could say or do anything else Higgins stepped between the two men, and suddenly Higgins was almost nose to nose with the agitator.

"Not a step further, Goulding. Don't you think I know you? We worked together at Hamper's not all that long ago. You were a trouble maker then and you've not changed now. But you'll not take one more step towards either Thornton or me."

"And how will you stop me, Higgins?" sneered Goulding, not retreating.

"I'm a union man. I'm on the committee, remember? The union might not be able to stop you from putting Hayleigh Mills to the torch tonight, but they'll run you out of town if you lay a finger on me." Higgins looked directly in the man's eyes, unflinching, while the two stared at each other in a battle of wills. After a few moments Goulding turned away, cursing as he threw down his torch onto the dirt road and pushed back through the crowd the way he had come.

With his departure the crowd lost its energy. Most of the men and women at the back of the crowd began to trickle away, disappearing down little alleys and past darkened doorways as Thornton, Margaret and Higgins watched silently. The men at the front of the group lingered a little longer, turning uncertainly back and forth as they glanced behind them at their diminishing numbers and then ahead at the silent observers. When a sortie of soldiers finally made a late appearance at the end of the street, moving rapidly in their direction, this last small number also dropped their torches and slipped quietly away. By the time the soldiers reached them, they found only Margaret sagging with relief in her husband's arms while Higgins stood awkwardly by.

Chapter Twenty

A Tremulous Hope

The days and weeks which immediately followed were the busiest that Thornton had ever experienced in his life. If managing one business was a full time job, managing a trust comprised of multiple businesses took more hours than there were in a day. Though on paper the separate mills functioned as one, in practical terms their owners were as competitive as ever, each jockeying for precedence and advantage over the others. Thornton had much ado to avoid favoring, or looking as though he were favoring, one owner above another, distributing the work evenly among all the mills and making sure that all were supplied properly for the contracts assigned to them. But he persisted in every detail. The thrill of meeting and surpassing a challenge had always run hot in his veins, and now that he had Margaret waiting for him at the end of each day, he did not have to be persuaded to leave his desk and go home when no more work could reasonably be accomplished.

The Thornton Trust, as it was called, was off to a fair start, though it had taken a little time to begin full production. Thornton refused to allow any items to be produced until he had first inspected and approved the raw materials to be used, accepting only those of highest quality and rejecting all others. He inspected all the machinery and drilled Higgins in the training of all employees, so that he was sure every worker followed the same set of procedures at every mill, and the finished product could be relied on for its consistency in every detail. He knew that the first impression made by the new trust on a buyer might well be the last impression, if it did not fulfill their expectations to the highest degree. When the first few orders had been produced and thoroughly examined, he sent them off and immediately began production on the next, waiting in fear and trembling to see how these first items would be received.

While this was going on Watson was making a slow but steady recovery. He was moved to Hayleigh just ten days after the Thornton's wedding, and shortly after that he was able to start answering questions related to the operation of Hayleigh Mills, which aided John considerably as he moved into his new responsibilities. It was not long before he began to learn what Thornton and Margaret had done to save his home and business. Watson was not a mean-spirited man. He was soon able to realize and appreciate the magnitude of what they had done for him and the town, and to soberly reflect on the folly which had led to such a necessity. In due time he expressed both his regret and his profound gratitude, and it was not long before a new bond of trust and respect began to spring up between Thornton and Watson. Never again would Watson delve into a new business venture without consulting his wife's brother, and Thornton appreciated Watson's efforts to learn from his recklessness and plan more prudently for the future.

It was just over three months after their wedding that Thornton came home a little early from the factory one afternoon and announced, with an air of satisfaction, "Margaret, I believe we can now manage to take the wedding trip we had planned out, if it is still something you would like to do."

Margaret smiled in her gentle way. "Is business really going so well, John?"

"Immensely well. I have had several large orders come in this week, the largest quantities yet requested, and all of them from repeat buyers. The trust is beginning to make a name for itself."

"Your customers must have been pleased with their previous orders."

"Indeed. They have expressed their pleasure with the new direction the Milton mills have taken, and they are willing to back up their words with their purses, knowing that their orders will not be delayed by needless strikes or labor troubles. In addition, we have cut down on the cost of shipping by sending all completed orders out in bulk, and this is adding to our profits."

"I am glad of it." Margaret's eyes glowed with pride as she looked at her husband. "The trust was certainly put in the right hands to be carried out well."

"The trust is working because, as you said, everyone has a stake in making it work. This level of cooperation is remarkable. It cannot last forever, of course, but it doesn't need to. If the debt can be repaid in the next year or so that is all the time we will need."

Margaret said nothing, but her face showed her pleasure and satisfaction. Thornton continued. "And so I thought, now that I know the trust is off to a solid start and Watson completely out of danger, we may as well take our wedding trip and have a celebration of sorts. Higgins and Daughtry can manage well enough in my absence for a short time. We can go to Bath next week and perhaps stay with your cousin for a few days after that before coming home. Would that be agreeable to you?"

"Very agreeable; but your mother is moving back to Marlborough Mills next week. Fanny decided today that she does not need any more assistance, now that Watson has begun to work in the office again each day."

"Fanny has not needed any assistance for a long time," Thornton scoffed. "She had more than enough servants to tend to her every whim from the time they returned to Hayleigh Mills."

"Some people are naturally more nervous than others," Margaret said gently, "especially under trying circumstances. I did not begrudge having to share your mother with Fanny, if that was what it took to give her some peace of mind."

"You are incapable of holding a grudge, love," Thornton told her affectionately, "which is one of your most endearing qualities. Will you come to Bath with me next week? I would rather go sooner than later.

There's no telling when something may arise with business to delay us again, and I'm sure that Mother would not mind us being away when she arrives. We have waited long enough already."

Margaret nodded, a small secret smile on her lips. She had every reason to believe that this would be her last chance to travel for some time, and hoped that she would have important news to share with her husband before they returned.

∞

The trip to Bath lost none of its sweetness for its delay. For four delightful days Thornton and Margaret were able to forget the responsibilities that lay so heavily on their shoulders and pretend that they had returned to the heady first days of their relationship. They were halcyon days, full of quiet walks among the shops, touring the grand gardens and homes, or attending concerts, but mostly simply enjoying each other's presence without the distraction of other people. Much was said and done during those days that would remain forever precious and sacred to the couple, too sacred to ever be entrusted to words. It was with the greatest of reluctance that they left the town at the end of their short time there, promising each other that they would return some day. After a short stop in town to see Edith and Mrs. Shaw, they returned to Milton.

In their absence Hannah moved home. She sighed with relief when the last of her belongings were brought inside the house, but she had to remind herself that she was no longer the mistress of Marlborough Mills. Though she knew Margaret would never abuse her privileges as the master's wife, Hannah recognized that it was now Margaret's place to arrange the menus, to decorate and furnish as she saw fit, and in general act as the lady of the manor. Nor would Hannah have wanted it any different. She could already see several small changes in the placement of tables and chairs and in the more subdued colors of flowers and vases displayed in the rooms; and she had to admit that some of the changes, at least, were an improvement over previous appearances. But it would still take some time to become accustomed to them, and not to feel as an interloper in her own home.

"It is good to sit here with you again, Margaret," Hannah said the morning after Thornton and Margaret had returned from their trip. The two women were together in the parlor while they worked on their sewing. Hannah was repairing a ripped hem on one of her dresses, while Margaret's lap was full of a flimsy white material that shimmered brightly even in the weak morning light of this overcast autumn day. Since the train from London had been rather late in its arrival the night before, this was Hannah's first opportunity to speak at length with the younger woman. "I hope you found your cousin and aunt as well as could be expected."

"They were very well, and happy to see us both. Little Sholto is becoming such a dear child. I wish you could see him."

"I do not care for traveling, so I will have to forego that privilege unless your cousin can come here. I am happy to leave all the noise and the inconvenience of arranging such things to younger, more adventurous people."

"I think you would enjoy Bath, if you are ever able to go. It is smaller than London, obviously, but much finer. There is a reason so many people flock to it every year. Even you might find its charms worth the noise and inconvenience once you were there."

Hannah shook her head. "Milton has more than enough charm for me, thank you. I will rely on you and Fanny to tell me what I miss by staying safely home, where I belong."

Margaret smothered an amused smile. "Speaking of Fanny, has she come to call on you since you left Hayleigh? She must miss you a great deal, having had you close at hand all these months."

"Not as much as you might expect." At Margaret's inquiring look, she continued. "Fanny has begun to take an interest in business affairs. She goes to Hayleigh Mills at all hours of the day on purpose, to be with her husband."

Margaret's eyes opened wide. "To be with Mr. Watson? I do not understand."

"Fanny says now that if *she* had been consulted while Watson was considering investing in the speculation, things would have turned out differently. She says she would never have advised entering into the venture if she had known what a weak foundation it had for success. As a result she now insists on taking part in any discussion pertaining to the mill's future." Hannah's tone indicated that she did not quite agree with her daughter on this point.

"Poor Mr. Watson! He has suffered enough without having his wife scold him for his failure."

"Oh, she doesn't scold him--quite the opposite. She coddles and fusses over him as if he were a child. He can scarcely move, in the house or out of it, without her constant supervision; but he seems to enjoy the attention. It's very convenient of Fanny to forget that she ever encouraged him in his ideas."

A passing cloud shifted the light from the window just then, and Hannah readjusted in order to see her stitching better. As she moved she could not help glancing up again at Margaret, marveling at the subtle changes she saw. The past four months had brought a new maturity to her daughter-in-law's face and added to the depth of her perceptive gaze, superimposing a stronger, wiser version onto the original image. Hannah knew by observation that Thornton was more content now than he had ever been in his life, and she was grateful for the younger woman's devotion to her son.

"You never told me how your family reacted to discovering that you had married John against their wishes," she commented, squinting into the light to thread her needle. "Were they terribly upset to get the news?"

"To be perfectly truthful, I don't know." Margaret gave her light, musical laugh. "They were welcoming enough when we met them on Harley Street in town three days ago, but they must have been shocked at first. I suppose four months was enough time for them to become used to the idea."

"But you must have some idea how they first responded," Hannah persisted.

"Not really. I can only go by the captain's reaction, after he arrived on the day Hamper's mill was burned down. His mouth hung open for nearly half a minute when the servant told him there was no Miss Margaret Hale, only a Mrs. Margaret Thornton, or at least that's what I was told."

"You did not see him when he came?"

"His train was delayed," Margaret explained. "Between the disturbance and the fire, the railroad had stopped all trains coming into Milton, and he had to sit in his compartment for several hours, unmoving, until the railroad decided it was safe to enter town again. By the time he arrived here John and I had already retired. He was disturbed to find that we were already married, but even more distressed to have missed his supper. But then the maid fed him what remained of the wedding luncheon, and all was forgiven."

"There is hardly a man on earth who cannot be managed easily enough on a full stomach," Hannah observed, with a knowing look. "After that I am sure he had no complaints to make."

"None at all. He went back to London the very next day, well rested and well fed, but it was still a week before I received two short, pointed letters of congratulations from Edith and my aunt Shaw. It took some time to settle their hurt feelings."

"Humph! As if Mrs. Lennox was in any position to dictate whom you should marry!" Dixon sniffed dismissively as she entered the room, a stack of freshly folded clothing piled high in her arms. "Her with her fine airs and graces! Some people do not know their own place." Hannah nearly rolled her eyes in response.

Of all the changes Margaret had already brought to Marlborough Mills, this was the only one of which Hannah thoroughly disapproved. Margaret had sent for Dixon to join her in Milton just two weeks after her marriage, but somehow, in all the fuss over the trust and Watson's health, nobody had remembered to mention her arrival to Hannah. It had been a shock to find Dixon installed as both maid and housekeeper upon her return to Marlborough Mills.

"That is enough, Dixon," Margaret said, gently but firmly. "It was only natural that Edith would want me to settle in London, preferably as her sister-in-law, but she has overcome that feeling. She is very happy for me now. And *you* did not always approve of me settling in the north! I'm surprised you agreed to live here again."

"Mrs. Hale would want me to be wherever you are, and that's the truth," Dixon said emphatically, making her way to the stairs. "I expect I'll get used to the Milton dust one day, and I'll do my best not to complain about living in such a dirty, noisy town again! But don't blame me if your laundry never comes out right!"

"The laundry will never come out well enough for *that* woman," Hannah said, looking exasperated, as Dixon's back disappeared at the top of the stairs. "Such impertinence in a servant! She feels free to comment on everything she hears. I wonder how you stand it, Margaret."

"Dixon has been with me all my life; I simply couldn't leave her behind in town. She is my last living link to my parents, except for Frederick, and if I have to deal with some impertinence now and then it is worth it."

Margaret's set expression and firm tone showed that there would be no moving her on this issue, and Hannah gave way with a dismissive sniff of her own. If Dixon were one of *her* servants, such bold statements would not be tolerated for a moment; but Margaret had her own ways.

"Whatever happened to your suitor, the Mr. Lennox your cousin wanted you to marry?" she asked, by way of changing the subject. "Did you see him while you were in town?"

"We did." Margaret frowned as the smooth fabric in her hands moved slightly, undoing the careful alignment she had just made. Sighing, she ripped out the basting stitches she had just placed and began again. "I think Henry is one of the reasons Edith eventually forgave me for marrying John."

"How is that?" Hannah asked, observing Margaret's struggle with her sewing for a moment. The object being held so carefully in her hands puzzled her. Whatever Margaret was making, it was very small indeed, and unusually fine.

"He has become enamored with a Miss Harriet Loudon, the daughter of one of the partners in his firm."

"Not *the* Loudons, of London!" Even in Milton Hannah had heard that name.

"The very same. It will be a good match for them both. She is a quiet, shy girl who admires Henry immensely, and he is happy to be of service to her whenever he can. Edith told me that Henry has realized he will do better with a woman who depends on her husband for every detail of life, not someone who is impulsive, independent, and given to speaking her own mind." The corners of Margaret's mouth tipped up as she said this.

Hannah gave a short, harsh laugh. "I am sure even your cousin realized you did not fit the bill."

"No, I do not. And of course if Henry marries Miss Loudon his rise to partner in the firm one day will be assured. It helps that Miss Loudon herself is quite charming."

"No doubt her money adds to her charms," Hannah said drily.

"By the time John and I arrived in town, Edith had as good as forgotten that she had ever imagined me marrying the captain's brother. She was very happy for us--and so was Aunt Shaw--and so was Henry."

Margaret had finished basting together the two tiny pieces of satin and now began, with tremulous hands, to attach a bit of dainty lace to serve as edging. Hannah continued watching, and as comprehension dawned her expression softened and her eyes took on a luminous quality. A look of immense satisfaction crossed her face, but she could not say anything before the door opened hastily and Thornton came striding in.

"I forgot one of my ledgers in my rush to leave this morning," he said by way of explanation, crossing the room and taking up the overlooked article as he spoke. He paused in front of Margaret. "How are you feeling today, love?"

"A little tired, but otherwise I am quite well." She offered up one of the tender smiles reserved only for him.

"And have you managed to eat anything today?" Thornton asked next, looking at her with fond concern.

"My stomach has settled and I was able to eat some bread a little while ago," Margaret assured him. "I will be sure to eat more after I finish this seam."

"If you need anything you have but to ask," he said, placing a gentle hand on her shoulder. Margaret reached up to grasp it with one of her own. "I will have to work late tonight, but I plan on checking in on you at supper." He looked at Hannah next, his expression becoming more serious. "I will depend on you, mother, to take the most excellent care of my wife for these next six months."

"She will have all the care that a mother can bestow on her child,"

Hannah responded with a fierce joy, and Margaret saw with relief that Hannah understood what she had been too embarrassed to say.

Chapter Twenty One

New Beginnings

The passing weeks and months were precious now, like the beads of a rosary fingered and prayed over fervently one by one. Autumn and winter could not disappear quickly enough for Margaret and Hannah as they waited and planned for the blessed event which was anticipated sometime in April.

Although Thornton was just as eager as they, he had a more mixed reaction to the falling of pages from the calendar. There were always rampant demands on his time and attention and not enough hours in the day to do full justice to everything that must be accomplished. After repeated conversations with Latimer and a lengthy meeting with all the underwriters, April was the time fixed for the complete repayment of the debt to the bank. If all went well, once the final amount had been settled and the payment disbursed, the trust would dissolve and he would be free to once more work for himself alone, without having to answer to anyone else. Besides this, he had an idea for a bold new enterprise, an idea which he mentioned at the dinner table one night in February, while he, Margaret and Hannah all ate companionably together.

"I have been thinking about what to do once the trust is dissolved," he started out. "I believe that it might be wise to attempt to branch out into new areas in the near future. I am increasingly uneasy with having all my business wrapped up in just one commodity."

"Are you growing weary of dealing with white fluff and looms all day?" Hannah asked, a little surprised by the announcement. He had given no hint of it beforehand.

"It is not a question of weariness; it is a question of security. As we saw last summer, having all the capital at one's disposal wrapped up in one product is risky; there is no room for error in such an arrangement. I am determined to improve our financial position by starting out in something wholly unconnected to textiles."

"What do you have in mind?" asked Margaret.

"I have been thinking about starting a newspaper," Thornton announced, as casually as if he were deciding what drink to have with dinner. Both women stared at him.

"I know such a move may surprise those who don't know me well, but I consider a newspaper as vital to a town as a school or a church. Reading the newspaper daily is an education all in itself, and the small paper we have now prints doggerel at least half the time. It is full of mistakes and shoddy storytelling, and often spends as much time retracting and correcting what it published last week as it does in printing today's news! A really fine paper, one dedicated to the business and civic concerns of Milton and the immediate area, would be a tremendous asset."

"What a splendid idea!" Margaret exclaimed, her eyes glowing. "A newspaper that would address the concerns of all the people who live in Milton! I know the paper must address business matters, but could you not use its pages to also highlight some of the daily struggles of the working people?"

"I knew you would think of them," Thornton's eyes softened as he looked at her. "If I do this, I promise you that the daily concerns of the workers and the poorest of the poor would find expression in every issue. I could do no less, with you to constantly remind me!"

"You would think of them anyway. You have always had a kind heart," Margaret replied staunchly, eager to praise her husband.

"You are a respected man in this town, John," Hannah said, looking at him with keen appraisal. "Many would be interested in hearing what you have to say on various matters. If you were to publish a paper I believe it would have an excellent chance of success."

"Right now this is nothing more than the roughest of rough ideas," Thornton said, nevertheless pleased by their immediate approval. "When the trust dissolves I will go back to producing cotton cloth on my own, and then I will investigate the idea further. Time will tell if it might turn into something useful; at present I have more than enough to occupy my mind." He and Margaret shared a significant look.

∞

On a rainy Thursday morning in mid-April, when the last of winter's chill had finally disappeared and the spring flowers were just beginning to raise their hopeful heads, Thornton did not appear on the floor of Marlborough Mills at his customary time. Looking down into the mill yard from one of the office windows Higgins saw that Dr. Donaldson's carriage was tied up in front of the Thornton home, and it was nearly impossible to focus his attention on work for the rest of the day.

Inside the house Dr. Donaldson had given strict instructions that only he and Dixon were to be allowed inside the room where Margaret now labored. Thornton sat at his desk in the parlor, mesmerized by the occasional sounds of footsteps and murmuring voices in the bedroom upstairs. He had chosen that location on purpose as it was the closest he was allowed to be to his wife during her hours of tribulation, and also because the proximity to his ledgers and other business items allowed the pretense of his carrying out work while he waited. In actuality he accomplished nothing. An occasional moan from Margaret caused him agony, and his hand stroked his chin worriedly uncounted times. Hannah sat rigidly on the settee across from him, fiercely attacking a sweater with a pair of knitting needles, while she too waited for the good news to be announced.

The time for the noon meal passed entirely unnoticed by either of the silent observers, though Hannah did call for tea to be served, which she and Thornton drank without tasting any of it. As darkness began to fall and the lamps were lit Thornton could no longer avoid showing his agitation. He stood and paced restlessly across the small room, straining in vain to hear any sounds from the room above. "It should not be taking this long, should it? Her pains were well established by the time we called for the doctor, but I have not heard any sound from Margaret in hours!"

"It is her first child, John. They generally take longer than others to make their appearance. You must not worry so." Hannah's calming voice did not match the tension in her hands as she gripped her needles. Thornton, still worrying, continued his pacing.

An hour later Hannah seemed to be vindicated by the appearance of Dixon, who descended the stairs calmly and looked at them both with an air of saintly patience.

"How is my wife, Dixon?" Thornton asked anxiously. He had stopped pacing the moment he saw the faithful servant. "Can you give us any news?"

Dixon raised her chin proudly. "Miss Margaret is doing as well as can be expected at this time. Dr. Donaldson said to tell you that, and he also asked me to fetch him a bite to eat." She disappeared into the kitchen without another word.

"There, John, you see what I told you." Hannah tried to soothe her son. "Sit down and relax. All is well. Dr. Donaldson would not be asking for food if the delivery were imminent. We may have quite a while to wait yet."

But Thornton refused to relax. A persistent fear that something was wrong had taken hold and began to gnaw at him. "Why would he not come down himself and eat here, if delivery is not to happen for a long time yet? Why can he not leave her side?"

"You worry too much, John," his mother chided, still knitting furiously. "Dr. Donaldson simply wants to keep an eye on her. Do not borrow trouble where there is none to be had!"

It was a quarter to ten, nearly three hours later, when Dixon again made her way downstairs, this time moving with a hesitant step. Thornton and Hannah both stood swiftly, hoping to hear an encouraging update, but their faces paled as they saw her wide, fearful eyes. "Dr. Donaldson sent me to speak to the master on his behalf," she began without preamble, looking straight at Thornton. "He would like your permission to try a new procedure on Miss Margaret."

Thornton's face paled even further, if that were possible; and he instinctively stepped closer, tempted to run straight up the stairs to his wife, instructions or no instructions. "A new procedure! What new procedure? What is going on up there? Why will no one say what is happening?"

Dixon took a deep breath. "The doctor says Miss Margaret's labor is stalled and no progress has been made for some time now. He says it is imperative to get the child out soon, or else risk losing them both."

For a moment Thornton could not feel the ground beneath his feet. He swayed where he stood; Hannah took his arm to steady him. No words would escape his mouth. It was Hannah who finally asked, "What is it Dr. Donaldson means to do?"

"I do not know, only that it involves some way of putting Miss Margaret to sleep. He said he saw it demonstrated in town last year and he has used it on other patients, but never on a laboring mother."

"Tell him to do what he feels he must," Thornton said, hoarsely, his voice finally returning, "only save my wife. Save Margaret!"

∞

The next hours went by in a blur. How many passed, Thornton would never know. He was conscious only of sitting in miserable silence, his head in his hands, whenever he was not up and pacing relentlessly back and forth across the length of the room. No comforting words from his mother could pierce his awareness, no smell of the food or drink she tried to press on him, though she took no sustenance herself. His entire awareness was in the small room upstairs, where his imagination played out many scenarios, each one more awful than the ones preceding. Not a sound penetrated from above, and to him, this silence was worse than anything. Laboring women usually cried out, did they not? Except for those moans in the morning, he had heard nothing of his wife's pains, and the worry ate at his soul.

At length there suddenly came a loud, extended cry that could only have come from Margaret; then a soft, mewing sound, like that of a newborn kitten, came cautiously down the stairs. Thornton and Hannah exchanged looks. The sound repeated itself, and then it grew louder--from a mew into a whimper, and from a whimper into the full throated wail of a newborn child.

"The child," Thornton gasped, heart pounding hard. He had risen to his feet without being aware of the fact. "The child is born!"

"Yes, that is the sound of your new son or daughter," said Hannah solemnly. "The ordeal is over--I hope." She looked at her son with wide eyes and could not say what he knew she was thinking. The question came from his lips instead:

"But Margaret--what of Margaret?"

By rights Thornton knew he was supposed to stay downstairs until summoned. The role of the father in these situations was to wait patiently while his wife and the doctor did all of the work, and then to be called in at the last to see what fate had fallen. But he could wait no longer. Ignoring all propriety he made for the stairs and took them two at a time.

Margaret's bedroom door yielded easily to his touch, and pushing it gently open he dared to look inside the darkened room. Now that he was here he felt as though he were trespassing on sacred ground, where angels might well fear to tread. He hesitated to cross the threshold, but nobody was paying him the slightest attention. As his eyes adjusted to the dimmer light he realized he was looking at Dixon's massive back, her frame standing between him and the bed where he knew Margaret must be. Dixon must have heard him enter, for she turned to face him, her expression both awestruck and tender. A miniscule white bundle lay in her arms and it was from this source that a child's lusty cry emerged once again. Dixon smiled tremulously. "You have a son, Mr. Thornton," she said, holding the child up a little in her arms so he could see for himself, "a fine, handsome boy!"

Thornton could spare only a moment to glance at his newborn child. "Margaret--what of Margaret? What has happened to her?" he gasped.

"Happened!" The doctor's voice emerged triumphantly from behind Dixon, on the other side of the bed. "Nothing has happened except that your wife has delivered a baby. And a strong, healthy child he is, too. Why, listen to him crying! There is nothing wrong with those lungs!"

"Margaret!" Thornton exclaimed, nearly pushing Dixon aside in his urge to reach his wife's side. "Tell me Margaret is all right!"

"She is perfectly well, though perhaps a little too sleepy to speak just yet," the doctor answered, with practiced fingers resting lightly on one of Margaret's wrists, and Thornton sagged with relief. "I used a little of the gas on her at the last. She was fighting so hard through every contraction that she could not make herself rest in between, and then she was in danger of wearing herself out completely. The gas relieved her pain and helped her to relax, which finally sped the process along. I have never tried this technique before in a laboring mother, and I am delighted with the results. Quite a remarkable woman, your wife!"

Thornton had no idea what Dr. Donaldson meant about using the gas, but he was not interested in finding out more just yet. Margaret's eyes were half open as he knelt next to the bed to take her other hand in his. There was a dreamy expression on her face but she smiled valiantly up at him. "Our son!" she half-whispered. "We have a son! I wanted you to have a son."

"I have you," Thornton answered, still shaken. "I have you, and that is all that matters. Are you quite sure you are well? You were so silent for so long, my love!" He clasped her hand tightly as he leaned down to kiss her, smoothing her hair and trying to convince himself that she was out of danger.

"She was just being brave, refusing to cry out, because she did not want to worry you and Mrs. Thornton!" Dixon broke in with her customary scolding tone.

"Only you could think about making *us* worry at a time like that!" said Thornton, framing his wife's face in his hand, heedless of the presence of others. "You are the bravest woman I know. How I love you!" He had to kiss her again, a gesture Margaret accepted until Dixon's voice broke in once again.

"Mr. Thornton, take this child and give him to Miss Margaret to hold for a minute or two. The least you can do is look at him together for the first time, while I prepare his first swaddling. He's as handsome a child as I've ever seen! Though he has the look of you about him, I think," she added somewhat grudgingly.

Later, perhaps, Thornton might remember to resent Dixon's impertinent words, or at least to laugh them off, but right now he had eyes only for Margaret--and his son. *His son*, he thought dazedly, as he took the small bundle from the servant's willing arms. In the grinding hours of waiting he had almost forgotten what the seemingly endless labor was supposed to produce. He felt more awkward and ungainly than ever before. Next to Margaret he had always felt large and clumsy, a rough, unpolished tradesman alongside a veritable princess; but now he felt positively afraid. The child was so small, so frail and yet so exquisitely perfect in every detail. Certainly *he* could have had nothing to do with the creation of this delicate miracle.

But Margaret did not agree. When Thornton had placed the child carefully in her arms she gazed down at him with all the tenderness of a Madonna before looking joyfully up at her husband. "He does look like you!" she said in wonder. "He has the same shape of face, the very same eyes! He is your son-- my little John!"

"Thank you so much, my darling wife!" The words were inadequate, but no others would come to Thornton just then. He leaned down once more, and this time it was his son's forehead that he kissed before bringing one finger up to stroke the back of a tiny fist. For long moments he and Margaret were motionless, gazing together at their son, who looked up at them with great blue eyes that seemed to be examining both his parent's faces. A discreet cough from the doctor finally caught Thornton's attention.

"Thornton, there is still some unfinished business with your wife. If you would please go back downstairs and tell your mother that she has a grandchild, Dixon and I can finish up what needs to be done here, and then I will leave you to your little family. Congratulations, sir," he added.

Thornton nodded, reluctant but willing to obey. His mother, he remembered, was still in suspense. "I love you, Margaret," he said aloud, kissing her one last time, caring not what the others might think. He turned away to leave, but the doctor's voice stopped him momentarily.

"And this time, Thornton, I will call you when your wife is ready to be seen." There was a smile in Dr. Donaldson's voice, which Thornton proudly returned before leaving the room.

Epilogue

Mr. Colhurst, the current majority leader of the House of Commons, left the Thornton house after a late dinner one evening some ten years later, having shared a meal with both the Thorntons and the president of the weaver's union, Nicholas Higgins. He had been a guest there many times before, but this time was different. On this particular night he had visited in order to congratulate the newest elected Member of Parliament, a certain gentleman from Milton whom he had cajoled into standing for the post only after that gentleman had been firmly convinced that he would never actually win; but in this he had been proven wrong. As soon as Colhurst had shaken his hand one last time and finally climbed into his carriage Thornton turned to face Margaret and Higgins.

"He looked altogether too smug for an M.P., in my opinion."

Margaret could not help herself. Thornton's face, so polite when speaking to Colhurst, had changed to one of an almost comical distaste. She burst out laughing and Higgins joined in with a wide grin. "You were the only one convinced nobody would vote for you in the by-election," Margaret said after a moment, still amused. "I always knew that you would be elected, and that you would be shocked when it came to pass. You underestimate the esteem with which you are held in Darkshire."

"I might not have agreed to his request if I had known there was a real danger of having to serve!" Thornton shook his head in evident disbelief. "Now I am locked into this for the next three years."

"It might be less time, depending on when a new election is called," Higgins responded, still smiling. "But I like the idea of you in office for three years. It's about time we had a friend of the union speaking on our behalf in the government."

"I will be representing all the people of Darkshire, not just the unions." Thornton's voice was suddenly serious. "But I will always be ready to listen to any concerns of yours, Higgins."

"I reckon you will. There's some men that always remember where they came from, no matter how high they rise. You're one of them."

"And you are another," Thornton rejoined. "You may be the head of the union now, but you will always be a Milton worker in your heart, where it counts. I may need to call on you for advice from time to time when there are business matters being discussed on the floor."

"I'll never forget what you did for me and mine when we needed you most. If there's ever anything I can do for you, you have but to say the word."

"I will count on you," Thornton agreed, and the two shook hands on it. With this solemn assurance made, Higgins likewise made his farewells, calling for his hired carriage to take him back to the same home he still shared with Mary and the six Boucher children, all of whom were turning out well.

"Higgins might have been speaking of himself just now," Thornton said reflectively, after Higgins climbed in and the carriage began to move away. "He will never forget where he comes from, no matter how many times he is re-elected."

"Have you noticed how much his speech has improved?" Margaret asked. "He will always have a touch of the common workers in the way he talks, but with all the interactions he has had with more educated people, the roughness has been wearing steadily away. In a few more years it may be gone entirely."

"I hate to think it would completely vanish," said Thornton with a grin. "Higgins without his accent would hardly be Higgins at all!"

The carriage had completely disappeared now, going around the corner and into the night, and by unspoken consent Margaret and Thornton turned together and walked back into the house, heading for the second floor. The hour was late and the children were probably already asleep, but it was a ritual their parents never overlooked.

"I still do not understand why Colhurst asked me to begin with." Thornton's voice was subdued, speaking almost to himself as they walked slowly together. "There are many more likely men already in public service who could have filled the role."

"But there is no one who knows business matters in this part of the country nearly as well as you. You have been publishing the most prominent newspaper in Darkshire for almost ten years now; you are aware of everything that happens in this county."

Thornton did not look convinced. Margaret continued. "And everyone knows of your efforts for the relief of the poor, which we have so many of just now. You are the ideal person to speak in parliament for measures for further aid. Perhaps you can convince them to have more railroad lines or other public works built. Your own rail construction has already taken several hundred names off the poor register. Mr. Colhurst could not have made a more ideal choice."

"I did not petition to lay a new rail line just to give employment to the people of Milton," Thornton answered earnestly. "I do not run charities. I did it because it made good business sense. Milton is centrally located between the mines in the north, the canals to the west, and the towns of the south. It was logical to take the profit from selling the cotton business and invest it in an industry which still has so much opportunity for growth. And I started it well before the cotton collapse."

"Nevertheless, it is your business sense that has enabled you to employ so many others."

Three years after their marriage Thornton had made the difficult decision to leave the business of cotton cloth production completely. His weekly newspaper, part news and part social commentary, had been increasing its circulation rapidly, and its growth required more and more of his time. Besides this, based on information from friends in America, he had become convinced that a civil war there was inevitable; and he surmised that a war in the States might have a detrimental effect on the supply of cotton needed for the continuation of his business. So he had sold the entire enterprise for a handsome profit and concentrated entirely on his newspaper for some time.

But the newspaper alone did not satisfy his drive to always be pushing into new ventures, and after a few more years he had formed a new investment group which petitioned for the right to lay new railroad track from Milton to the north. After some time and considerable opposition, the permission had been granted, and miles of new track were already in place when the sudden fall in cotton's fortune had occurred. So Thornton was a master again, this time employing hundreds of workers who might otherwise be standing in line at one of the numerous soup kitchens that now dotted the landscape of northern England.

The ever-faithful Dixon met the Thorntons coming up the stairs just as she was going down. "Are the children asleep, Dixon?" Margaret asked as they passed by her.

"Nearly so, except for young master Thornton. He's a curious child, that one! Mrs. Thornton, bless her heart, has been answering questions from him for this half hour at least."

"What sort of questions?" Margaret asked, prepared to be amused; for she knew that little Jack, as he was called, possessed an imagination that knew no bounds, especially when he was trying to put off going to sleep. Hannah, more indulgent with her grandchildren than she had ever been with Thornton or Fanny, was often hard put to know how to stop his relentless queries.

Dixon rolled her eyes. "When Mrs. Thornton and I started putting them to bed, he wouldn't lie down at all at first. He wanted to go to sleep standing up, just as his papa's horses do, he said. But that wasn't all. He asked me where the dark goes in the morning when the sun comes up, if you can believe that, and by the time I left the room he was asking Mrs. Thornton how we can all be God's children if God hasn't any wife."

"Oh dear. That sounds like it might take all night to answer." Beside her, Margaret felt Thornton's suppressed amusement.

"That's his goal all along of course, and poor Mrs. Thornton can't abide denying him anything. He'll keep her talking till morning if nobody puts a stop to it!" Dixon shook her head disapprovingly and continued on her way downstairs.

"Jack has always reminded me of your father, with his constant desire to learn," said Thornton, chuckling as Dixon moved away. "Nevertheless, I will speak to him rather firmly in the morning. There is a time and place for everything."

"It still seems odd to hear Dixon refer to your mother as 'Poor Mrs. Thornton'," Margaret replied in an undertone as they approached the nursery. "It's clear to see that some sympathy has built up between them at last."

"Children have a way of bringing out the best in people. Dixon and my mother are both devoted to the children, and their common interest has given them common ground." Thornton laid his hand on the door of the nursery just as Hannah opened it from the inside, lamp in hand.

"They are nearly asleep," Hannah told them, speaking quietly. Apparently she had finally gained the upper hand with her grandson. "You might rouse them again if you go in," she warned. But she stood back to allow them to enter, knowing the ritual as well as anyone else in the house did. Thornton and Margaret advanced into the room and saw their three sons nestled closely in for the night. Benjamin and Charles lay with eyes closed, breathing evenly, but Jack's eyes, still as blue as the day he was born, were just drifting shut. They opened wide when he saw his parents, and Thornton moved closer and placed a calming hand on his namesake's shoulder. The child half-smiled as sleep claimed him, and then his eyes slid shut. Thornton and Margaret left the room as quietly as they had entered, noting that Hannah had already gone to her own room.

"Do you want to look in on Bessie as well?" Thornton asked his wife as he let the nursery door close silently behind him.

"No." Margaret shook her head. "The nurse will wake me later, if necessary. I am hopeful that our daughter is starting to sleep through the night. I would rather not take a chance of waking her up if we can avoid it." Thornton made no objection, instead offering Margaret his arm in order to lead her to his room. They had shared Thornton's room every night since Bessie's birth six months earlier, allowing Margaret's room to be used for the infant and her nurse instead.

As they began their bedtime preparations, Margaret could not help thinking of the changes that would inevitably result from Thornton's new position. "I suppose we will have to move to town?" she asked, more a statement than a question.

"I'll look into renting a townhouse tomorrow," Thornton promised her, resigned to his fate. "Hopefully we will not need it for long."

"What do you think your mother will say about moving? You know how attached she is to Milton."

"She is also attached to our children," Thornton reminded her, "and for their sakes, I think she might be willing to make the transition. But with Fanny finally expecting, she might decide to stay there instead and help her as long as needed. I will ask her tomorrow what she would like to do."

"I am so happy Fanny and Watson are finally going to be parents," Margaret commented, her face showing her satisfaction. "For so long it seemed as though it might never happen."

"You should see Watson when he is in the newspaper office,"

Thornton told her with a grin as he slipped his night shirt over his head. "He can speak of almost nothing else. You would think nobody had ever been an expectant father before. He will be completely insufferable once the child arrives, I think." Watson had followed Thornton's lead, sold Hayleigh Mills, and thrown his lot completely into the newspaper as well, working as an editor under Thornton's direction.

"It seems a shame we won't be here when they become parents," said Margaret, sounding wistful. Thornton stopped his movements and looked at her carefully, then came around the bed to take her hands in his.

"My love, we do not need to go to town at all if you would rather not. I do not have to serve. I only ran as a favor to Colhurst after all."

"Absurd, to think that you could overthrow the wishes of the people who voted for you! No, John, I insist that you fulfill your responsibilities, and the children and I will be there to support you while you do so. It will be good for them to grow up in town with their own cousins, little Sholto and Maria and Claire, even if it is only for a few years. And then we will come back to Milton."

"Do you think so?" Thornton asked thoughtfully. "I can see where you might become too enamored with town to ever want to return."

"Nonsense. As I told you when we married, you are a part of Milton and it is a part of you. This town is in your very blood, and I could not have one of you without the other. We will most certainly return here some day!"

"Thank you, love." Thornton said, moved as he always was when she made such bold professions of her devotion, and he kissed her gratefully. After extinguishing the lamp he folded back the bedspread and then climbed in under the cover of darkness. When Margaret joined him her pulled her close, enjoying her warmth as she snuggled next to him. She sighed contentedly as she laid her head on his shoulder.

"John?"

"What is it, love?"

"I am thinking about that phrase you used just now, common ground. I think I might use it as the title of my next article for the paper. It describes the theme perfectly." It was an open secret in Milton that Margaret contributed heavily to the articles published by her husband, particularly those articles which promoted social reform.

Thornton made an indistinct sound, which Margaret took to mean he was considering the idea. She continued. "There are so many conflicts between masters and workers which could be resolved much more easily if both sides would simply try to find common ground."

"It is wise advice for everyone, not just masters and workers," Thornton answered, his arms tightening around her. "We had our own share of conflicts at one time--do you recall? We had to find our own common ground before we could come together."

"John, you promised me we would not dwell on those unhappy memories ever again!"

"They were not *all* unhappy." Thornton gently turned his wife so that she was facing him. "Put your arms around me, love, as you did on the day of the riot." Margaret willingly obeyed, and Thornton continued speaking as he held her close. "I will never cease to be amazed that you and I were able to come together despite our differences, and to be grateful that I have had your love all these years."

"I feel the same," Margaret whispered in the dark, and kissed her husband with an eagerness that had not diminished but only grown over the years. "My own dear John!"

"My own dearest Margaret!"

THE END

About the Author

Elaine Owen is the pen name of a married mother of two who discovered Elizabeth Gaskell's _North and South_ in 2015 and immediately had an urge to continue the story. In her spare time she enjoys music, martial arts, and advocating for people with disabilities. _Common Ground_ is her fourth published work. You can contact Elaine at ElaineOwen@writeme.com or through her "Elaine Owen, Writer" page on Facebook.

If, like Elaine, you are also a fan of Jane Austen, you may enjoy one of her _Pride and Prejudice_ variations: _Mr. Darcy's Persistent Pursuit_, _Love's Fool: The Taming of Lydia Bennet_, and _One False Step_, all available on Amazon.

Printed in Great Britain
by Amazon

51059605R00088